CAPTURED

THE CAPTIVE SERIES BOOK 1

ERICA STEVENS

BOOKSHELF

Books written under the pen name

Erica Stevens

The Coven Series

Nightmares (Book 1)

The Maze (Book 2)

Dream Walker (Book 3)

The Captive Series

Captured (Book 1)

Renegade (Book 2)

Refugee (Book 3)

Salvation (Book 4)

Redemption (Book 5)

Vengeance (Book 6)

Unbound (Book 7)

Broken (Book 8)

The Captive Series Prequel

The Kindred Series

Kindred (Book 1)

Ashes (Book 2)

Kindled (Book 3)

Inferno (Book 4)

Phoenix Rising (Book 5)

The Fire & Ice Series

Frost Burn (Book 1)

Arctic Fire (Book 2)

Scorched Ice (Book 3)

The Ravening Series

The Ravening (Book 1)

Taken Over (Book 2)

Reclamation (Book 3)

The Survivor Chronicles

The Upheaval (Book 1)

The Divide (Book 2)

The Forsaken (Book 3)

The Risen (Book 4)

Books written under the pen name
Brenda K. Davies

The Vampire Awakenings Series

Awakened (Book 1)

Destined (Book 2)

Untamed (Book 3)

Enraptured (Book 4)

Undone (Book 5)

Fractured (Book 6)

Ravaged (Book 7)

Consumed (Book 8)

Unforeseen (Book 9)

Forsaken (Book 10)

Relentless (Book 11)

Legacy (Book 12)

Coming 2021

The Alliance Series

Eternally Bound (Book 1)

Bound by Vengeance (Book 2)

Bound by Darkness (Book 3)

Bound by Passion (Book 4)

Bound by Torment (Book 5)

Bound by Danger (Book 6)

Coming 2020

The Road to Hell Series

Good Intentions (Book 1)

Carved (Book 2)

The Road (Book 3)

Into Hell (Book 4)

Hell on Earth Series

Hell on Earth (Book 1)

Into the Abyss (Book 2)

Kiss of Death (Book 3)

Edge of the Darkness

Coming 2020

Historical Romance

A Stolen Heart

Special thanks to my husband and best friend, my parents, siblings, nieces and nephews who make life more interesting and fun, and Leslie Mitchell from G2 Freelance editing for all her hard work.

CHAPTER ONE

BLOOD SLAVE.

The words were enough to send a cold chill of terror down Arianna's spine. She shuddered, swallowing heavily and repeatedly, as she tried to wet her suddenly *very* parched throat. Her lips were sore; she could taste her dried blood upon them as they were chapped and cracking.

She'd had nothing to drink in hours, she was thirsty, and her mouth was dry as cotton. The fire that consumed parts of the forest had burned her throat, and she could taste the ash on her tongue.

The smell of smoke clung to her, cloying in its acrid odor. She would give anything for some water, but she was fairly certain her misery and discomfort would soon be coming to an end anyway.

The dead did not require water after all.

Surprisingly, the thought of dying aroused less fear in her than the alternative of becoming a blood slave did. Though the notion never entered her mind before, she realized she'd prefer to take her own life before such a thing happened to her.

The thought of being kept, of being trapped and used for the most disgusting means known to man, was enough to make her want to rip out her hair and run screaming in horror.

She did neither, however, because she couldn't move enough to carry out either action. She was trapped, surrounded, penned in by the bodies crammed against her. The raid on the encampment in the woods was successful. The temporary homes of many ripped apart, destroyed, then set ablaze. Their lives were irrevocably ruined; they would never see their loved ones again.

The fortunate ones, the ones who weren't chosen to be blood slaves, would be bled outright. Their blood would be drained unwillingly, and painfully, from their bodies. A hundred separate needles would pierce their skin before they were finally killed.

The blood would be bottled and saved for later use. The unfortunate ones, the blood slaves, would be used over and over again until their owner became tired of them and either sold them off or bled them dry.

Aria hoped she would be chosen to be bled dry. She would rather feel the sting of a *thousand* needles than be repeatedly used for months or years. However, she had a feeling if the vampires found out who she was, they would never allow her such a compassionate death. They would never grant the merciful end she fervently hoped for.

She glanced at the people surrounding her. She knew they would all willingly die before they revealed her identity; she also knew she was a complete idiot for allowing herself to be captured in the first place.

If these monsters ever found out who she was, they would have strong leverage over the rebellion and her father. They would try to use her against the rebels living in the woods, hiding, moving, and fighting the vampires who relentlessly hunted them. The vampires who had taken their world and twisted it into a cruel mockery of what it once was.

2

At least that was what she'd been told happened.

She didn't remember a world without starvation, hiding, and death. She didn't recall a world where food was purchased in stores, and homes were heated and cooled. She knew a world of woods and caves, of hunting and struggling for her meals.

She knew a world that was either brutally hot or deathly cold, a world where there had never been a consistent roof over her head. A world where her father was the leader of the rebel movement, her mother was dead, and her two brothers were being trained to take over their father's position one day.

She'd never experienced a life of safety and security, never experienced a life where she wasn't fighting and running daily. She'd heard the stories of the world before the vampires ruled, and though she was sure some of the tales were wrong, she still thought that world sounded amazing compared to the reality of this one.

As a child, she foolishly pined for that world. As an adult, she threw aside childish dreams in favor of learning how to fight and hunt. Instead of dreaming of a world that no longer existed, she learned to survive.

After childhood, hugs stopped being exchanged amongst her family, and the only praise she received lately was for her far superior skills with a bow and arrow. However, though love wasn't freely given, she knew it was there, and it was strong.

Her brothers would risk everything to get her back; her father would want to do the same, but he would also know it couldn't be done. No matter how much he'd *want* to, he couldn't risk the lives of so many for one person, even if she was his daughter. It would kill him to lose her, he would make the sacrifice, just as he had sacrificed so much else in his life.

No, she had no grand ideas of salvation. No dreams her brother, William, would charge recklessly in to rescue her, yelling like a banshee, just as he charged so wildly into everything he did.

She didn't have these dreams because her father, and the ever-sensible Daniel, would never allow William to do such a thing. They would probably have to tie him up just to keep him away. He would hate it, but it would be the only way to keep him alive.

A twinge of regret and sorrow filled her at the thought of William. He was her twin, her other half. They had been nearly inseparable since conception. He would never get over this, just as she never would have gotten over his loss if their roles were reversed.

She never should have allowed herself to get caught. But then, she hadn't had a choice. The child...

Aria's gaze slid to Mary Beckins. Mary stood proudly, her shoulders thrust back, her chin jutting out as she stared unblinkingly across the sea of heads before her. If it weren't for the tears streaking silently down Mary's dirt and soot smeared cheeks, Aria would have thought her fearless. Even with those tears, she still looked proud, defiant... unbreakable.

Seeming to sense Aria's stare, Mary's eyes slid toward her. It was Mary's child, John, whom Aria had saved. It was John's place she took in this cramped hell of near certain death and deprivation.

Aria had forfeited her life for young John's, and she would do it again if she had the choice. She just wouldn't have been so reckless about it. She wouldn't have plunged in carelessly, and she would have at least tried to think of a way to ensure she and Mary weren't caught too.

Like her twin though, she rarely thought out her actions and often charged thoughtlessly forward, heedless of the consequences. But these were by far the direst consequences she'd ever faced, and they would also soon be her last. Or so she hoped.

Mary held her gaze for a moment; gratitude filled her brown

eyes. She briefly nodded her thanks and managed a tremulous smile Aria returned.

The vampires didn't know who Aria was, or who her father was, and she was certain no one who knew her here would tell them. The people had always respected and admired her father, but today, with her actions, they had also come to admire and respect her too. They would all die before they handed her over, even if handing her over meant a pardon on their lives and a chance at freedom for themselves.

"Worry not, girl."

She tried to turn to see who had spoken to her, but she couldn't move against the crush of bodies pressing against her. She could smell the dirt, the sweat, the fright, and smoke adhering to all of them. Life in the woods didn't allow for regular bathing. She was accustomed to body odor, but this was far more intense than what she was used to.

She didn't know if it was because they were all so confined when they were used to wandering free, or if it was the inevitable end of their lives making their odor exceptionally acute.

Either way, the stench was overwhelming. She wanted to gag on it or cover her nose and attempt to block it out. She wanted to cry, but she stood frozen by the paralysis of revulsion gripping her.

Sudden movement drew her attention back to the stage set up before them. A *stage* for crying out loud. It wasn't humiliating enough to be packed in like this, but they would also be paraded forward, separately examined, and chosen from the specimens presented. Aria shuddered again as she struggled to keep her composure in this swiftly unraveling, and entirely unfamiliar world.

"Be brave, Aria, be brave." She swallowed heavily, managing a small nod as the man behind her whispered in her ear again. "Take strength from those around you."

Aria fought back the hot wash of tears flooding her eyes. She straightened her shoulders, refusing to show weakness, refusing to break in front of the monsters now lining up before them.

As long as she was selected for death, she could remain strong through this. She *would* be as brave as her father and brothers would be in this situation. She would never give the vampires the satisfaction of seeing her break; she would die with her pride firmly intact.

There was a ripple of movement amongst the imprisoned crowd. Aria realized the gate had opened, and they were starting to pull out people. She watched in disgust as they removed the first person and led them up the stairs to the stage. She didn't recognize the young woman, who openly sobbed as she was paraded before the line of monsters eagerly eyeing her.

Behind the stage, other vampires had gathered on the street leading through the heart of the town contained within the massive walls surrounding the distant palace. The vamps were crammed in between the two and three story buildings lining the street as they eagerly strained to see the fresh human meat.

The enormous walls, offering protection for the town nestled within them, enclosed nearly four square miles of land around the palace. The richest, the aristocrats of vampire society, resided within the walls, lavishing in their lives of opulence and brutality while the humans they enslaved suffered at their greedy hands.

She *despised* them.

Every part of her, every cell in her body, hated every single vampire within these palace walls as well as outside of them. The only thing she hated more was the humans who had betrayed their kind to reside in relative freedom amongst the ruling class of vampires.

On the mountain, rising above the town like an avenging demon, the imposing palace loomed over them. She'd seen it before, it was impossible not to notice its glistening turrets and golden spires from the treetops, but she'd never been this close to the enormous structure before.

She hated to admit it, but the palace was impressive and beautiful as it glimmered in the muted rays of the sun. She hated it terrified her as much as it did, but she couldn't shake the overwhelming sense of doom as she gazed at the massive, elegant structure housing the biggest monster of them all, The King.

Unable to look at it anymore, Aria tore her attention from the palace. Her attention drifted down the hill behind her. Beyond the outer palace walls, scattered towns were situated within the valley nestled below. Those towns housed the human, servant traitors and vampires who weren't as wealthy as the ones gathered on the street across from her.

Her people starved, they froze to death in the woods and caves. They fought to retain a freedom that was elusive, and brutal, while their kind betrayed them, and the captured fighters were brought here to be humiliated, tortured, and sold.

The gathered vampires watched the proceedings with an air of indifference that left Aria fuming. It was bad enough they'd been caught, and were considered no more than food, but did they have to be treated as if they were worth less than an animal?

Actually, most animals she came across were treated far better than this as they were necessary for human survival. Aria's hands fisted at her sides; her jaw clenched as she fought to keep control of her volatile temper.

She watched as a woman was led to the side. The woman bowed her head; her shoulders shook with the force of the tears as she was led onto the stage. The woman's clothes were little more than rags, though Aria knew her clothes weren't much better. For that matter, neither was her hair or overall appearance.

Due to the hunting party, she'd been with before being

captured, she'd gone longer than usual without bathing. The lingering scent of blood, body odor, wild animal, and death stuck to her. They didn't blend so well with the other awful smells encompassing her. She found herself hoping her dismal appearance and stench would be enough to earn her the much-coveted sentence of death.

A boy was brought forth next, then a shirtless young man who was well muscled from hunting and working within the forest. The man wasn't led over to the boy and woman but escorted over to a vampire.

A young woman came forward to claim him, or at least she appeared young; there was no way to know her real age. She was tall and thin, with a hawkish face both brutal and strangely beautiful.

The vampire woman eagerly eyed the young man; the look in her eyes caused Aria's legs to shake. It was more than apparent what the woman was going to do to him. She wasn't going to wait long either as she hastily led the man off the stage and through the crowd gathered on the street. The crowd leered after them as they disappeared.

Aria wasn't sure she would make it through this. She understood now the woman and boy on the stage were destined for death, something the boy also seemed to realize as he began to weep.

The muted sound of sniffles began to make their way through the rest of the crowd. The majority of people remained strong, but it would only be a matter of time before they were also broken beneath the heel of the monsters now holding their fate.

More people were brought forth. The compression of bodies around her eased, if it weren't for the tense pressure in her chest, she might have been able to inhale easily again. Instead, she could barely breathe through the panic threatening to crush her.

Most people were slated for death, but it was the ones chosen to be blood slaves who sobbed the loudest. Aria was panting for breath when someone stepped beside her. A work-worn hand slipped into hers and squeezed it reassuringly.

Turning toward the person beside her, Aria felt like she'd been kicked in the teeth when she saw him. "Max," she breathed.

CHAPTER TWO

MAX MANAGED a wan smile for her. His clear blue eyes were sad and resigned, yet they still resonated with the strength and confidence she was used to from him. The sight of him here was nearly her undoing.

A sob rose then caught and strangled in her throat. Max and her brother Daniel had been best friends since they were children. They were always together; nearly as inseparable as she and William. Max was like another big brother to her, teasing her, taunting her, teaching her things, and protecting her.

He'd also been her first crush as a girl; before she came to understand there would never be a place for romantic love in her life. She realized a while ago she wouldn't have a long life. It certainly wouldn't ever be a peaceful or safe one.

There was no way she would ever bring a child into this world of brutality, oppression, and humiliation. And now she wouldn't even have a choice in the matter; her lifespan had been drastically shortened on this day, and she could almost hear her time ticking away.

However, for one brief year, when she was still a young, silly

girl, she entertained thoughts of a home and a family. Max had been the man at the center of most of those fantasies.

And now he was here, with her.

"Max," she whispered again, her heart shattering into a thousand pieces.

She hadn't thought things could get any worse; she was mistaken. Her death was fine, she could handle it, but to know Max might die too, or even worse *survive*, was more than she could tolerate.

Max had always been kind, patient, and gentle with her. She'd given up her fantasies of one day being with him, but she still loved him. She couldn't handle this too, not bravely. Not anymore.

He tilted his head; his eyes surveyed her as his jaw clenched. "Stay strong Aria, stay strong. Think of your brothers, your father. We *will* get through this."

"How did they catch you?" she mumbled miserably.

He didn't have to answer her though, she already knew how. She and Max were both with the hunting party when it came upon the human camp. The vampires were already there, raiding the recently assembled camp with ruthless brutality.

They initially rushed to aid the people, but it quickly became apparent it was going to be a losing battle, and they would be of no use. The best hope was to flee, retreat deeper into the woods, and hide until the vampires withdrew with their new captives.

That was what they were doing when Aria spotted young John being detained; she'd plunged heedlessly forward to intervene on behalf of the young, scrawny boy. And she'd cost her father and brothers two of their best soldiers.

"Oh, Max," she whispered, and fresh tears filled her eyes.

"I couldn't let you come alone. Plus, I've always been curious about what happens here." He tried to sound light, but she heard the tension in his voice. "Don't cry for me, Aria, they'll

think you're crying because of them, don't give them that satisfaction."

"They'll keep you," she moaned, knowing it was true.

Even filthy and disheveled, his handsome features were visible beneath the layer of dirt covering his face and bare chest. It took Aria a moment to realize not only was Max bare-chested, but so was every other teenage and middle-aged man within the pen.

A vise clenched her chest; they'd been stripped of their shirts to entice higher bids from the females. Aria supposed she should feel thankful they allowed her to remain fully clothed, but all she felt was nauseated.

"That will give me a chance to figure out an escape plan for the two of us."

"No, Max, they won't keep me. I have nothing to offer them."

It was true; she was skinny, dirty, disheveled, smelly, and unwomanly in every possible way. They wouldn't choose her, or at least she clung to that hope. They didn't appear to be picking blood slaves solely on looks alone, but rather some strange method she didn't understand and didn't want to. She didn't aspire to have any understanding of the monsters holding their fates.

"I'd rather be dead anyway," she assured him.

His blue eyes filled with displeasure; a muscle jumped in his cheek. "They will pick you, Aria, and when they do, you have to cling to the knowledge I will come for you. I *will* save you. Remember that, it will get you through the awful times ahead of us."

The heartfelt emotion radiating from him staggered her. "Max—"

"I will come for you, Aria. I promise you that. I *will* find a way to come for you."

She gasped, stunned when he was suddenly ripped away

from her. It was only then she realized there were just a handful of people left within the fenced holding area. She almost chased after him, and the creature pulling him along, but she only made it one step before she halted abruptly.

She couldn't show that much emotion here; they would only use it against her, or Max. No, she had to remain in control, had to be as emotionless as she could, or they would use her love to destroy them.

Max was paraded onto the stage and promptly claimed by a vampire woman who oozed sadism. Aria's mind spun as she realized the fate Max was just handed. He believed he would escape, and she knew he was wily and strong, but *no one* ever returned to the woods, and freedom, after vampires captured them. Once a person was taken, they remained a prisoner until they died.

Max was now at the mercy of this woman, and as long as she possessed him, the vampire could do whatever she liked to him, and for as long as she chose to keep him alive. When she grew bored of him, she would kill him, or sell him, and then come back here for another toy.

Aria's legs trembled, and only sheer will kept her upright.

She didn't fight the rough hands seizing her; she was in too much shock to fight right now. Max was going to be used and tortured, and it was her fault.

Why hadn't she listened to her father when he told her to use her head, to think before acting? Her foolishness hadn't only destroyed her life, but the life of one of her best friends.

Self-hatred curdled through her. She didn't care what happened to herself anymore, or what they did to her. Led through the crowd, they brusquely pushed her onto the stage where they paraded her before the horde of vampires gathered there. Then, they trudged her passed the vamps packing the streets.

It appeared the vamps on stage had the first choice, and the ones on the street received the second pick to grab the goods if they chose. Aria was dragged back past the people on stage and pulled roughly around, but no one claimed her.

She didn't feel as relieved as she thought she would. If Max was here because of her, then she should suffer the same tormented fate he did; it was only fair she wasn't granted the merciful death she'd been hoping for.

She met Max's gaze briefly, hating the dread and helplessness in his eyes as she was pulled back toward the street side. This would be the last chance for someone to claim her, and if they didn't, she was fairly certain Max would go ballistic in his attempt to save her.

Aria's heart hammered in her chest; she could barely see through the waves of adrenaline and terror crashing through her. She blinked as she stared at the street, hardly noticing the man who stepped forward.

"I will take it."

It! It! Aria's mind screamed, she recoiled in dismay at the word. The thing who claimed her was moving through the crowd, digging into his pocket to retrieve the money he would spend on her. He wouldn't be spending much, as she was almost on the chopping block before he claimed her.

He was an ugly thing, but then they were all nasty, twisted, and cruel to her. But this one was hideous, with stooped shoulders, pointed nose, and severe hazel eyes. He looked warped, evil; wrong.

The coppery tang of blood clung to him as he stepped forward and roughly grasped her chin. Aria winced; she tried to jerk away as he turned her head sharply back and forth, but he would not release her.

"She may be fun for a bit, easily broken."

Aria tried to remain brave, but she could feel a shattering of her soul that was far more distressing than anything she'd ever experienced before. And she had suffered some disturbing things in her life. But this, *this* was the worst.

This man was going to do many, many things to her. None of them would be good, and all of them would be designed to savage her body, toy with her mind, and break her. She tried to believe he wouldn't succeed in breaking her but judging by the perverse gleam in his eyes, she wasn't so sure he wouldn't.

Money exchanged hands; the two vamps holding her released her to the man. She felt the urge to flee, to run screaming down the street, but she wouldn't get far, and she would *not* give them the satisfaction of seeing her snap.

The vamp began pulling her toward the stairs, not at all caring she could barely keep up with his far faster gate. She staggered, trying to keep her shaking legs beneath her as he reached the stairs.

"Wait!" A deep voice boomed across the crowd gathered within the street and echoed off the surrounding buildings. It rang with authority and a note of command that stopped even Aria abruptly in her tracks.

The vamp holding her froze instantly, his hand loosened upon her arm, but he didn't release her. There was a rippling amongst the throng, murmurs filled the air but were swiftly silenced as the crowd stepped aside to reveal a tall man standing in the middle of the street.

Well, not a man, but rather one of her most hated foes.

He stood casually, his broad shoulders thrust back and an impassive look on his face. His tousled black hair fell about his hard face in waves that highlighted his dangerous good looks. Looks Aria tried not to admire, but she found herself doing so as she drank in the sight of him.

The dark glasses on his well-defined nose completely shaded his eyes and covered a quarter of his face. The dark blue shirt he wore hugged his upper body and revealed a hint of the carved muscles ridging his abdomen, chest, and biceps.

His hands, folded before him, rested on the head of a cane with a silver handle she couldn't see. At his side sat a gray wolf. The wolf's eyes were bright emeralds and eerily focused on her as it sat motionlessly.

Behind the man stood two other vamps, but Aria barely paid them any attention as the fascinating creature who disrupted the proceedings made his way forward. The tip of his cane clicked faintly on the cobbled streets as the wolf padded at his side. As they approached the stage, the wolf moved in front of him, brushing against his legs before climbing onto the stage.

The man, however, didn't make a move to come onto the platform where she stood. The vampire who had claimed her, and still grasped her upper arm, finally broke the profound silence.

His voice quivered as he spoke. "Prince... ah, your Highness?"

Aria's mouth parted with a small puff of air as she took in the powerful stranger with new eyes. She didn't know much about the vampire stronghold, but she'd heard rumors of the creature who would one day rule all their fates if his father ever died. She'd mostly heard he was as cruel and heartless a bastard as his old man.

Aria straightened her shoulders, a wave of defiance washed over her as she clenched her jaw and lifted her chin. She didn't know what came over her, but her apprehension vanished in the face of this man, and now she was angry. Pissed actually, royally *pissed* by the inhumane and unfair treatment of her fellow man.

The wolf brushed against her, and though he startled her, she kept her surprise hidden as the animal settled at her feet with a small thump of his tail.

The vamp holding her shivered; his trepidation became almost palpable as the prince remained unmoving and silent.

Apparently, the rumors she'd heard about the prince were true, as everyone seemed to be fearful of the creature before her.

The prince's mouth quirked, amusement flitted briefly over his striking features. Behind the thick glasses, she could feel his attention riveted on her.

"She will come with me," the prince stated.

A collective exhalation escaped the crowd, but the sharp looks of the two men behind the prince silenced them. The auctioneer sputtered somewhat, his eyes darted to Aria, then around the rest of the stage.

"Your Highness, we have others..." he broke off, looking frantic and confused as he searched the crowd for help that wasn't forthcoming. "Better looking and cleaner ones."

Aria shot the auctioneer a dark look he didn't notice as he was too focused on the intimidating man at the foot of the steps.

"Ones who I am sure will be far more to your liking. I will select one for you if you would like," the auctioneer continued to gush.

"No," the prince responded. "I am taking *her*. Give the man his money back and give her to me."

The man holding her released her instantly; he couldn't seem to get away from her fast enough as he hastily retreated. Dread trickled back through Aria. All these people were terrified of the prince, and he was now laying claim to *her*.

What did that mean? What did he want with her, and why on earth would he choose her when the auctioneer was right, there were far better-looking women here?

Aria turned toward Max. His eyes were wide; his nostrils flared with the force of his rapid breaths. Terror was written all over his face; however, it wasn't terror for him, but for *her*.

Aria shuddered, her hands clenched her elbows as she hugged herself. She found herself oddly undaunted by the prince before her, but she was scared of the reaction everyone else had to him.

"Come here," the prince commanded.

She jumped a little at the sharp command, but she found her feet frozen in place. The auctioneer was gaping at her like she was a total moron, but she couldn't bring herself to walk. Finally, having decided she must be a complete idiot, the auctioneer stepped toward her and reached out to grab her arm.

"Do *not* touch her!"

The auctioneer stumbled backward as the prince's barked command rang out. The auctioneer went deathly pale; sweat poured down his face as he gaped at her. His reaction finally snapped some sense into her.

She couldn't stand here all day. The prince would only come for her; he did own her now, and she didn't know what he would do if he were forced to retrieve her. There were other innocents on this stage, and Aria worried the prince would hurt them if she continued to disobey him.

Max stepped forward. She shook her head at him, terrified of what would happen if he tried to stand up for her. This whole mess was her fault, and Aria had to accept the consequences, no matter how dire they may be. The wolf moved away from her as she stiffly made her way down the stairs.

The prince followed her movements; he stepped back as she stopped before him. Her reflection stared back at her from the dark lens of his glasses. It relieved her that she didn't look terrified, even though she was a trembling mess of confusion on the inside.

He was large, powerful, overbearing, and despite her intense hatred for him and all his kind, she couldn't help but acknowledge he was also magnificently handsome.

Why would he choose *her?*

He remained unmoving, his gaze focused on her for a

poignant moment. Then, he abruptly turned away, leaving her bewildered and motionless. She didn't know what to do, what was going on, what was expected of her. Her gaze slid helplessly back toward Max. His jaw was locked; disbelief and astonishment were evident on his face. He turned toward her, his bright blue eyes fearful.

'I'll find you,' he mouthed silently.

Aria would like to believe him, but she didn't see how she could escape the powerful monster who owned her now. How could she escape the palace?

Maybe, if she'd gone to one of the homes in the town she would have a chance, but she couldn't begin to fathom a way out of that monstrous place. She shuddered, her fingers dug harder into her elbows. The wolf slipped past her and plodded after his master.

"This way."

Aria jumped at the forceful command, but her feet felt as if they were stuck in mud. The two vampires who accompanied the prince came toward her, their hands outstretched.

Aria stepped back, frightened by their massive size and callous eyes. The prince turned back, his dark eyebrows furrowing together over the top of his glasses as his full mouth pinched sternly.

His men seemed to sense his sudden irritation as their hands fell limply back to their sides. Aria gawked at the prince, startled to realize he appeared truly irritated by the idea of them touching her.

"Move," one of the vamps commanded gruffly.

The prince didn't turn back around as he strolled down the street. The wolf and the three of them trailed behind.

CHAPTER THREE

ARIA COULDN'T GET her mouth to close for more than a few seconds at a time. Everything was so astonishing and *strange*. She had never seen anything like this, had never imagined it could even *exist*. And now she stood smack dab in the middle of it, being openly stared at and whispered about as she was ushered into the vast, rambling entry hall of the massive palace.

She'd heard stories about the palace's exquisite beauty and intricate designs. She'd always assumed they were just that, *stories*. She'd never dreamed such a breathtaking, opulent place could exist, let alone that she would be walking through it.

Everything was sparkly and bright, huge and wonderful. There wasn't a speck of dirt or dust anywhere; she didn't even see a smudge or footprint on the floor.

She glanced at the rounded roof far over her head; her mouth parted even more as she took in the astonishing artwork on the domed ceiling. She'd never seen anything like the beauty in the colors and detail of the designs above her. She'd never even seen a painting before.

Daniel loved to sketch when he wasn't busy hunting for food, planning attack strategies, or fighting for his life. He created amazing things with the charcoal they scavenged from the caves, but his creations had no color, and they were nowhere near as large and spectacular as this.

Dropping her head, she hurried across the white, sparkly floor. She was ashamed she found anything amazing and beautiful here, embarrassed of the awe filling her, but she couldn't help it. It was so different from her woods, so different from the life she knew and loved. There were even designs within the floor, swirling streams of gold and silver fluidly entwined together.

"Braith!"

Aria's head snapped up; she tore her attention away from the floor to the woman striding purposely toward them. Dressed lavishly, the woman's golden hair was pulled back in a braid that emphasized her beautiful features.

Aria stopped, unable to move or breathe as she stared in disbelief at the stunning woman. A woman who had never known hunger or fear, or been made to dress in dirty rags, a woman who stared at her with open animosity.

"*What* is this?" she demanded coldly.

"It's a blood slave, Natasha," the prince replied dryly.

The woman blinked in surprise, her gaze raked disdainfully over Aria. Though Aria wanted to shrink from the woman's scathing look, she managed to throw her shoulders back, narrow her eyes, and hold the woman's gaze. The prince didn't look at Aria but simply stared at the woman.

"I can see that, Braith. What are *you* doing with her?"

Aria stared defiantly at him as he turned to survey her from head to toe and back again. She refused to let them see the anxiety coiling through her. She couldn't forget that all this beauty was home to some of the worst evil the world had ever known, and at the moment, she was in the middle of it.

"What is normally done with a blood slave, Natasha?" he inquired, his deep voice rumbling out of him. "I thought you would be happy I finally decided to take one."

Am I the first slave he's ever taken? Aria wondered.

But no, that couldn't be possible; these creatures loved their blood slaves. They loved to torture, use, and abuse people until there was nothing left of them. It was what she'd always been told, so it had to be true. Didn't it?

"You could have cleaned her up first. She's a mess, Braith; I cannot believe you brought her into our home like this. I could smell her from a mile away, and she probably has lice."

Dislike shot through Aria, her hands fisted at her sides as she glared at the blonde woman. She may not be at her cleanest right now, but she most certainly did *not* have lice.

"I will take care of it immediately," the prince said.

Aria's glare turned toward the prince. There it was, that awful "*it*" word again. She was most certainly more than an "*it*," but she wasn't in here, she wasn't in this place. She was fairly certain she might never be more than an "*it*" again. The realization infuriated her, and more than anything she itched to show them exactly what she was capable of, and it was far more than being an "*it*."

"I should hope so," the woman retorted.

The woman brushed hastily by them, leaving Aria glaring after her and fuming over the conversation. A subtle nudge from the wolf alerted her they were moving once more. She hurried forward, eager to catch up with the prince, suddenly terrified he would leave her alone in this place.

A place she wasn't welcome in at all, a place that didn't seem nearly as magnificent as it had two minutes ago. How could she have forgotten, even for a moment, where she was, and every horrible thing this place represented?

She didn't care to think about the fact that the only thing making her feel safe in this strange world was the creature who now believed he owned her. It was far too disturbing a thought, and she didn't understand why she would feel that way.

He'd done nothing to earn her trust, and she knew beauty was only skin deep, but she found she had a tentative belief her fate wouldn't be any worse with the prince than with the ugly little creature who first claimed her.

Aria's hand trailed across the ornate, shiny wood of the railing as they moved leisurely up the massive staircase. They had stairs in the caves, where she spent a fair amount of her life, and she had spent time in abandoned houses, but none of those stairs were anywhere near as elaborate or large as these were.

"Gather some female servants." The prince barked the command over his shoulder as they reached the balcony running around the second floor.

One of the men broke away, heading in the opposite direction down the long hallway before disappearing down another set of stairs. Despite her intentions not to be impressed by the things she saw anymore, she couldn't stop the amazement sparking to life within her again as she viewed the hall.

She didn't know what she wanted to look at more, the beautiful works of art lining the wall on her left, or the fantastic room to the right. She had just walked through the grand foyer, but it was more stunning from up here. The thousands of pieces of glass in the chandelier reflected a multitude of bright colors from the mural above it and onto the floor.

The open balcony ended abruptly as walls enclosed them once more. Aria was trapped within this world of decadence, greed, brutality, and death. Max planned to rescue her but she didn't hold out much hope for it, just as she didn't hold out much hope she would find her own escape.

She couldn't even remember how to get out of this vast place, never mind try to escape from it or get away from the monsters living within it.

For the first time, genuine concern for her life took hold. She'd been too stunned, too upset and confused to grasp the reality of her situation. It was sinking in now, and it wasn't good. Her heart raced in her chest and pounded against her ribs.

She folded her hands before her as she tried to remain as docile and inconspicuous as possible. Not like it would do her much good, she didn't hold out hope they would forget she was there, but they didn't need to know she was more dangerous than they suspected.

They didn't know who she was, she reminded herself. She wouldn't be punished because of that at least, and maybe one day she'd get the chance to use it to her advantage.

Her thin build would also help her appear weak. She itched for her bow, but the two brutes who took her down had stripped it from her. She still had her speed, and her deftness; they couldn't take those from her.

If she remained docile, then maybe they would let their guard down around her, and she would get an opportunity to escape. It was a slim hope, but it was the only one she had to cling to. What she didn't like to think about was what would happen to her in the meantime.

The guard with the prince stopped before a door, swung it open, and stepped back to allow the prince entrance. Aria hesitated within the hall, her hands folded before her as she stared into the darkened room. The prince didn't turn on a light as he disappeared into the shadows with the wolf trailing him.

The remaining guard stared unkindly at her, his dark eyes

burrowing into her. Then with his cold voice, he murmured. "Go."

Aria prickled at the command. She had the urge to turn and run down the hall. It didn't matter if she didn't know how to get out of here, she didn't care anymore. She couldn't just walk into that darkened room and give herself over to a fate worse than death.

Aria backed up a step as the man started toward her. Panic tore through her; she felt like a cornered animal as she came up against the wall. A large hand came at her; Aria instinctively knew if it touched her, she would lose control of whatever composure she had left.

"I have made it clear *no* one is to touch her."

The threatening words growled from the doorway of the dark room, caused the hair on Aria's neck to rise. Her gaze traveled toward the prince. He had returned to the open door and was leaning against the frame, but the tension in his body belied his casual posture.

"If I have to tell you again, I will kill you," he stated.

Aria's mouth dropped, her heart flipped crazily, she could feel the powerful beat of her pulse fluttering rapidly in her neck. She didn't know what to make of this whole, awful, bizarre situation.

The man stared at the prince as if he had sprouted another head. His gaze darted to his outstretched hand before he dropped it to his side and stepped away from her. She didn't blame him; she wouldn't want to be anywhere close to her either after that threat.

"Come inside." The prince ordered.

Aria glanced around the hall. Running was still a tempting thought, but she couldn't disgrace herself in such a way, and she was pretty sure being tackled by a member of the royal family would be pretty disgraceful.

The prince had told the man not to touch her again, but that didn't mean *he* wouldn't come after her, and she had a feeling if the prince had to chase her down, it wouldn't end well. She gathered her rapidly diminishing courage as she stepped uncertainly toward the darkened room.

The prince stepped away from the door, blending within the shadows again for a moment before light flooded the room. Aria was unable to suppress her astonishment. Without thinking, she gradually moved forward, drawn by the beauty and splendor of the lavish room. She took in the artwork and stunning hand-carved furniture.

She tried to look everywhere at the same time, to see it all, but there was far too much to take in at once. Large bay windows, with a cushioned seat, overlooked the most picturesque gardens she'd ever seen. Flowers bloomed and spilled everywhere, ornamental trees were scattered throughout, and it all flowed forth in an endless wave of color.

She loved her woods, savored her time within the dark interior and massive trees, but what they lacked in color, this garden made up for in spades.

The paintings within the room were all of landscapes, scenic mountains, and rivers with animals and sunsets so realistic she felt like she was looking at the actual place. Handsome lamps, colorful and clear vases were spread throughout the room. The three sofas within looked inviting, and their deep green color reminded her of the ivy she loved in the groves of the forest.

Aria took a few more steps forward, unable to close her mouth as she tried to absorb as much of the beauty as she could. She found herself more than a little overwhelmed and wholly enthralled by the splendor surrounding her.

For a moment, she didn't know worry or starvation; all she knew was beauty, peace, and a sensation of amazement so profound she could barely breathe.

The soft click of the door drew her attention back to the prince and the harsh reality of her life now. Beautiful things may surround her, but the vilest *creatures* roaming the earth also surrounded her, and one of their leaders was fixedly watching her.

He remained by the door, his hands enfolded over the head of his cane. The wraparound glasses hid his eyes, but she could feel them on her as his full mouth pursed and his eyebrows drew together.

Aria blinked at him in surprise, only then realizing tears rolled down her cheeks. Worried he would think her tears were because she was afraid, she wiped them hastily away.

Straightening her shoulders, she defiantly met his gaze. His forehead furrowed in consternation as his head turned unhurriedly around the room. Aria frowned at him, unable to understand the strange expression on his face, or what caused it.

A faint knock on the door drew both of their attention behind him. The prince opened it and stepped back to allow three women into the room. Aria's nostrils flared as she took in the women. They were all human, she could tell by the drab servant's clothing they wore, and she hated them even more for it.

These were the people who abandoned their kind; who had given themselves over to the vampires in exchange for not having to fight or stand up for themselves. These were the people who would rat out their fellow human beings in a heartbeat if it meant furthering themselves.

Most human traitors were amongst the servant class, but a few had risen to higher and more valuable positions on the deaths staining their souls. Aria glared at the women, her hands fisting and un-fisting as she fought the urge to punch them.

These types of people caused her mother's death. They had infiltrated the camp, garnered trust, and turned them all over. Her mother was murdered during the resulting raid.

Aria clenched her jaw as she struggled not to launch herself at one of these women as they pulled the door closed behind them.

"You sent for us, milord," the tall blonde said. Her eyelashes fluttered obnoxiously at the prince as she all but offered him her vein.

He nodded toward Aria. "I would like her cleaned up."

Aria bristled as she turned her animosity on the prince. She was not a dog for Christ sake; she was perfectly capable of bathing and cleaning herself. She most certainly didn't need the help of these "*women.*"

Three sets of eyes slid toward her; curiosity radiated from them as they fully noticed her presence amongst them. The blonde eyed her with open abhorrence, the redhead seemed utterly indifferent, but the pity in the small brunette's eyes truly incensed Aria. She didn't want any pity.

She turned away, unable to look at them any longer. They repulsed her more than she repulsed them.

"Of course," the blonde purred.

"I will have clothes sent up for her at once," the prince said.

Aria tore her arm away when someone touched her elbow. "Don't touch me!" she snarled, feeling no remorse when the redhead shrank away from her.

The three women eyed her warily, apparently trying to decide if she would be a danger to them, something that might be a possibility.

"You will allow them to clean you," the prince ordered.

"I can clean myself!" Aria snapped.

The women gasped, shrinking farther away from her as she deliberately, and loudly, defied their leader. She didn't care; she was frightened and outraged and more than a little tired of being treated like something worse than an animal. She was entirely at the mercy of the vampire standing across from her, staring at her as if she were something he'd never seen before.

She supposed he wasn't used to being defied, and she also supposed such defiance often resulted in severe consequences, but she would prefer punishment rather than this humiliating experience. Just an hour ago, she'd been hoping for death; now she found she was probably on the verge of it.

The prince stepped toward her, using his massive size to try and intimidate her. Aria clenched her jaw as she glared at those thick glasses. She hated that he wore them. She wanted to see his eyes when she told him to screw off.

He stepped closer to her, giving her no choice but to retreat if she wanted to avoid him touching her. And she most certainly did *not* want him touching her. She edged further back when he pushed closer, nearly bending over her as he loomed above her.

"Stop it!" Aria hated herself for crying out in protest, for letting him see how much he rattled her, but she couldn't stop the words as her heel came up against the back of the wall and she realized she was trapped.

His hands slammed into the wall on either side of her head, rattling the pictures. Her heart lurched as, for the first time, she feared this creature. Until now, she hadn't known what to make of him, or what he planned to do with her.

She now knew he didn't take well to being defied, and she was a little concerned he might rip out her heart—something he could do before she could blink.

"You will allow them to do this, or I will do it for you," he growled.

Aria gulped at the terrifying possibility he would do what he threatened. She had no doubt he would drag her into the bathroom, strip her, and dump her into a tub of water. There was no way she would allow something like that to happen.

Unfortunately, she didn't respond to him as quickly as he

apparently would have liked. He grabbed her arm, practically dragging her from the room. Aria hurried to keep up with him, stumbling behind as he pulled her forward.

He led her through a side door; she caught a brief glimpse of books, a desk, and leather chairs before she was pulled into yet another room. This one left her bewildered and gaping. There was some strange, overlarge round white thing in the middle of the room. Its golden handles gleamed, and some sort of spigot came from the top it.

He released her abruptly before striding across the room. He spun the handles, causing water to burst free from the spigot. Aria's hand flew to her mouth. What kind of brilliant, strange contraption was this?

The prince turned toward her, confusion marring his brow as he studied her.

"Oh," Aria breathed as steam rose from the water, alerting her to the miraculous fact the water was hot.

She'd seen the bottom of these things in a couple of houses before, but there were no spigots with water coming from them. Most of the bottom parts were broken, or so dirty she would never contemplate stepping foot in it, never mind using it to clean herself.

She hadn't known this was their intended use, and it fascinated her. It was rare she had time to boil water to fill the few wooden tubs they hid within the caves. Most of the time, she didn't bother because of the effort it took, but every once in a while she treated herself to a warm bath in a tub instead of the lakes or streams.

The prince was studying her; the perplexity on his face more than a little disconcerting. She couldn't meet his gaze as an unexpected wave of shame washed over her. He was studying her like that because he realized she knew nothing of the world outside of caves, woods, streams, hunting, and death. And he pitied her for it.

As she looked back at him, she didn't see pity on his face. Instead, she saw an understanding that left her rattled and unsure. She couldn't figure out this strange creature, but it seemed as though they were even, because judging by the look on his face, he couldn't figure her out either.

"Allow them to do this," he said gruffly.

Aria nodded before he left the room.

CHAPTER FOUR

Aria shifted as she tugged at the collar of the sweater she wore. It was a velvety type material, and she had never felt anything like it. It felt marvelous against her skin, but she couldn't get used to it. Her clothes were always rough, ragged, and nowhere near as warm as this soft cloth.

She tugged at the scooped collar again, unnerved and frightened by how much of her skin it exposed. Even in the summer, she wore long sleeves and collars to avoid bug bites, scratches, and other hazards amongst the woods and within the caves.

The sweater, though strange, wasn't as bad as the skirt they put her in. It fell to just above her knees in gentle black waves that swayed as she walked. She didn't like the feel of it or the fact her legs were exposed. Usually, she slept fully clothed in case there was a raid. It was essential she always be quick on her feet and able to flee if it became necessary.

Wearing this, she wouldn't be able to move fast, and would almost inevitably be caught as the sweater was a bright red homing beacon to her location. The women had scrubbed her clean, had done the strange task of removing the hair from her legs with a razor, but they couldn't take away the bruises and scratches marring her skin.

She looked ridiculous in the skirt, with her battered lower limbs and knobby knees. The garments were uncomfortable but preferable to being nude as they'd taken her clothes away, with the blonde snickering something about burning them.

The women fluttered around her, brushing her hair as they talked. They hadn't said a word to her, nor had she spoken to them for the past few hours. They exchanged gossip, spoke of men they liked, and whispered reverently about the prince. From all their excited chatter, Aria learned the blonde fancied herself amongst the prince's favorites.

Aria tried not to think about the discomfort and confusion that revelation caused her. She should be relieved the prince had other women to keep his attention; maybe he would just take blood from her and nothing more. That thought was repulsive enough, but until she could escape, she might be able to bear it.

Aria winced as the blonde, Lauren, nearly tore her hair out at the roots from brushing it far too roughly. Aria glowered at her, but the woman scarcely noticed as she continued her assault on Aria's hair.

"When was the last time you brushed this mess?" Lauren muttered.

Aria clenched her jaw and hands, refusing to answer the vapid woman. The brunette, Maggie, gave Aria a sympathetic glance as she finished applying some strange color to Aria's nails. She stared at them in confusion, not understanding why anyone would like to do that to their nails; but apparently, it was popular as all three of the girls wore it.

Julia, the redhead, brought forth a pair of shoes Aria was certain were designed to kill her. Who walked in such a high and pointy shoe anyway? Whose ankles could take those things?

Aria remained still as they applied their final touches and

stepped back to examine her more closely. Aria's gaze slid away from them, hating the bite marks marring their necks and inner wrists. It was apparent they willingly, and from the way they were talking, *eagerly* gave their blood away.

She wondered if it was the prince they gave themselves to as they seemed at ease in his place, or if they gave themselves to any vampire who asked.

"Why do you think he chose her?" Julia inquired, tilting her head to study Aria more closely.

"I don't know; she's most certainly not anything to look at. The prince must have decided it would be good to have a blood slave available to him whenever he was hungry," Lauren replied. "Though we're always available."

Julia giggled; her eyes sparkled as she covered her mouth with her hand. "Yes, we are."

Aria managed to keep her face impassive, she itched to smack the insipid women, but she forced herself not to react to any of their catty words. Aria felt she was no competition for the voluptuous women, but it was more than apparent Lauren felt threatened by her for some reason.

Aria wasn't going to reassure her that she didn't have to be concerned Aria was competition; she wanted nothing to do with this place or its people.

"Bony little thing," Lauren muttered.

Aria bit back her sharp retort. Julia knelt before her and thrust the tortuous shoes onto Aria's feet. She winced as her foot was twisted and crammed into the awful, cramped monstrosities.

When Julia finished, she grasped Aria's arms and helped her rise. Aria cringed, hating the uncomfortable things now strapped to her feet. She stood, wobbling and uncertain, and trying not to grimace in pain.

"You will get used to them," Maggie told her, patting her arm reassuringly.

Julia and Lauren rolled their eyes but decided to keep their snarky comments to themselves for a change.

"The prince is waiting," Lauren said.

Aria tried to adjust to the new shoes, but she could barely move in them as she crept forward at an annoyingly slow pace. There would be no escaping in these awful contraptions, and she cursed the idiot who invented them.

Maggie took pity on her and grasped her arm, helping her to walk. Aria didn't jerk away from the girl, mainly because she required the help, but also because no matter how much she disagreed with Maggie's choices, she almost tolerated her.

Led back into the main room, she discovered the prince lying on one of the sofas; his large body took up most of it. His arm was tossed over his eyes, and he had one leg planted firmly on the floor.

The wolf lay on the floor before him; the animal lifted its head to watch as they entered the room. The prince must have sensed them as he dropped his arm and sat up. He still wore his glasses, but Aria knew the moment his eyes landed on her. Her heart flipped in her chest; a strange sensation trickled through her as he stared silently at her.

"Leave us," he commanded.

The three girls nodded briskly before slipping from the room. Aria stood uncertainly, her hands folded before her and frightened by what was going to happen next.

"Much better," he murmured. "Come here."

Aria bit her bottom lip. She hated the way he made her feel so frightened and nervous, but at the same time, strangely excited. Apparently being captured had frazzled her mind as she found herself oddly unafraid, and more than a little curious of the man who purchased her.

"I won't harm you," he said.

She didn't know if she *should* believe him or not, but Aria felt she *could*.

She attempted to totter forward on the death traps strapped to her feet. A small cry escaped when her ankle twisted out and her legs buckled beneath her. He was beside her instantly, catching her before she hit the ground.

Aria stared at him in surprise as he lifted her effortlessly. She didn't understand this strange creature before her.

Vampires were monsters, they destroyed humans, used and abused them before tossing them away, but this creature was an enigma she couldn't begin to fathom. One moment he was over-bearing, intimidating, and threatening. The next he was almost kind as he held her gingerly in his grasp.

Was this part of his game? Did he plan to try and gain her trust before tormenting and eventually destroying her? That explanation seemed far more likely than the one where this crea-ture, one of the leaders of the monsters, might *be* kind.

"I don't think those shoes are for you," he commented dryly.

Aria eyed him warily as he settled her onto the sofa he had just abandoned. "Most definitely not," she agreed.

Startled disbelief filled her when he knelt before her. Her breath froze in her chest as the prince of the vampires leisurely slipped the awful things from her feet. His hands were soft on her; his touch caused an odd thrill to race up her spine. She found herself wanting to trust him, wanting to *like* him even.

And she knew that was a very dangerous thing to do.

BRAITH STARED at the young girl before him. Her eyes were as big as saucers, unblinking, completely bewildered as she gazed at him. His hand brushed the supple skin of her leg. The dark bruises and scratches marking her were vivid against her fair complexion.

He didn't know what caused the apparent abuse she'd withstood, but he didn't like it. Not one bit. He didn't know what it was about this girl, but she intrigued him in a way no one ever had before.

She was a pretty enough thing with the layers of dirt scrubbed from her body. She smelled better now that the smoke, blood, and stench of body odor had been removed. Braith detected a faint hint of strawberries clinging to her hair, even though they'd washed her in some flowery scent that didn't suit her.

This girl wasn't one to be wreathed in fragile flowers. He sensed that beneath her outward, docile demeanor there was something far stronger than the way she was trying to appear. Her natural scent, despite the floral clinging to her skin, was a great indicator of that fact.

Her features were pleasant, delicate even, but not refined. Her parted mouth was full, her teeth straight, and surprisingly white for the lack of hygiene she displayed upon arrival. Her crystalline blue eyes were full of disbelief, trepidation, and uncertainty. They also appeared intrigued as she tilted her head to study him.

Her hair, scrubbed free of grime, was not a lackluster brown like he initially believed, but a glossy dark auburn that gleamed in the light of the room. The red streaks within it were lustrous. He wasn't sure he'd ever seen a shade quite like it.

Though she was far from ugly, he still didn't understand what had driven him to claim her. He'd seen women far more beautiful women than her in his extended lifetime. She was too skinny, her collarbone stuck out sharply, and the bones in her hands were visible.

He preferred his women with more meat on them, but from

the look of her, it was apparent her life wasn't one of abundance and pleasure like the women he was used to.

From the moment he'd seen her, actually *seen* her, he was consumed by the need to have her. There was nothing spectacular about the stage setup, or the people on it. In fact, he hadn't seen a single person on it until she was brought forth.

He hadn't planned to stop at the auction. He had no use for blood slaves. There were enough willing people in the world without having to take blood from the unwilling ones, but when she was led across the stage, he'd stopped dead in his tracks.

She had been unremarkable, filthy, disgusting, and bold. Defiance and pride had radiated from her. They were a beacon calling out to him, snagging his attention as nothing in years had. At first, he barely saw her, but the longer he stared at her, the clearer she became to him.

He sat back now, tilting his head as he watched her. She studied him with the same intensity with which he studied her, but they considered each other for entirely different reasons.

She wondered about her fate, what he was going to do with her, and what he sought from her. He studied her because he could actually *see* her. It was not only utterly mind-boggling to him, but also a little disconcerting.

"Why are you being so nice to me?" Her melodious voice was low, her forehead furrowed as her gaze ran over him.

Braith tossed the nuisance heels aside before he rose to his feet. Her lips parted, her head tipped back to stare at him. "What is your name?" he inquired.

She licked her lips nervously; her small hands pulled at the sleeves of the sweater as she fidgeted anxiously. There were small nicks and cuts on her fine-boned fingers; calluses marred the palms of her tanned hands.

"Arianna."

He lifted an eyebrow. "Is that your real name?"

A small smile flitted over the edges of her full mouth, for the first time he saw humor in her eyes. "Yes."

He believed her as he settled onto the sofa beside her. Though she tensed, she didn't move away from him. "I'm Braith."

She nodded, her gaze distrustful again as she looked him up and down with shrewd and assessing eyes. "So I've heard. Why am I here?"

"I don't know yet, Arianna."

Trepidation flashed through her eyes; she recoiled before insolence blazed hotly from her.

"Everything you do to me will be done by force," she declared.

Her defiance should annoy him (she'd already defied him more today than anyone *ever* had in his life), but he found himself somewhat amused by it. If no one else was around, he didn't mind her show of courage. He wouldn't tolerate it in front of others again though.

"You think so?" He was far more interested in seeing her reaction to his words than her actual response.

She looked surprised but quickly covered it up. "I know so!" she retorted sharply.

He shrugged indifferently. He didn't know what he wanted with her or what he was going to do with her. He may decide tomorrow he didn't like her here at all; Braith didn't believe he would, but he was known for his whims of fancy when it came to women. He was fascinated by the reaction he had to her, but there was no way to know how long that fascination would last.

One thing was for sure, he wasn't going to force himself on her. He had done a lot of things in his long life, many of them not good, but he had never forced himself on an unwilling woman.

"We shall see," he stated.

Her delicate nostrils flared with fury; he could hear her teeth grinding. He didn't know why he was baiting her, but it was amusing to watch her when she was irritated with him.

"Where are you from, Arianna?"

Though she still held the appearance of defiance, he could sense the grief shimmering through her. "Around," she said.

"You live in the woods?"

"Yes."

"Are you a member of the resistance?"

She hesitated, her knuckles turned white. "That's why I'm here, isn't it? Resistance members are punished for their disobedience by becoming blood slaves, or bled dry. It's a way to discourage our fighting, isn't it?"

"I suppose so," he agreed. "You think that's wrong?"

"Don't you?" she snapped.

He sat back and leisurely stretched his legs out as he folded his arms behind his head. The bright blue of her eyes blazed with anger and righteousness as she glared at him. It pleased him to smile serenely back at her.

"If your kind would simply just agree to work with us, then punishment wouldn't be necessary," he said.

"Agree to be your slaves in other ways you mean? Agree to be your servants? Agree to do whatever you wish, whenever you wish it, with no regard for our wants, desires, and beliefs?"

The fevered tone of her voice and her impassioned words fascinated him. For someone so young, she was very firm in her beliefs. Without thinking, he reached out and seized her hand. The urge should have staggered him, but there was something about the gesture that seemed right, as did the warmth of her hand within his.

Her heart sped up as he tried to soothe the tight pressure of her fists by running his thumb over her knuckles. Her head tilted to the side; those large innocent eyes were surprisingly earnest as she watched him.

"It is the law of the world that the strongest prevail," he informed her.

"And you are the strongest?"

"Of course."

She tried to pull her hand free, but for a moment he held onto it. He finally relinquished it to her when she turned away from him and focused on the wall, apparently determined to ignore him. He wasn't about to let that happen.

"You do not agree?" he prodded.

Her head bowed as she fidgeted with the sleeves of her sweater again. "You did succeed in driving us out of our homes, forcing us to run and hide. You do feed off us, and you have certain attributes that make you *physically* superior. So yes, I suppose that makes you stronger. In *your* minds at least. It doesn't give you the right to do what you have done to us."

"Many people returned to their homes when the war was over. Many people picked up the lives they left behind. It is only the resistance who remained hiding and fighting and dying in the woods for the past hundred years."

She turned back to him; her defiance melted away as indignation blazed forth. "Is that what you believe? They simply picked up exactly where they left off? They returned to something good? That they have been thriving since the war ended? Even within the woods, with no walls, and no real homes, we have more than the ones who returned to their *lives*.

"They are starving, with little clothing and no money. There were no jobs to return to that didn't involve being some servant to your kind and being beneath *you*! There was nothing for most of them, as they were forced into menial roles meant to keep them stupid, and weak, while building *your* kind and *your* world to ever higher levels.

"I've heard there was a time when there were schools, when we were taught things and educated. They do not exist anymore;

they are things of legend, whispered about in awe, as so many other things are. Things we used to have and enjoy, but will never again know if *your* kind has anything to do with it!

"There is survival of the fittest, and then there is cruelty. I may pay the price for my role in the resistance, but I wouldn't change a thing. I stood up for what I believe in, I have pride, and no matter what you do to me, you can't take it away!"

There was genuine wrath in her voice by the time she finished speaking. Her hand trembled in his as she had unknowingly seized his hand with both of hers. The fervor in her voice, the conviction with which she spoke, was almost enough to make him understand her plea, her cause.

But he knew the way of the world, and the way of the world was that only the strong survived. He found it unfortunate her people were relegated to such roles, but it was necessary to ensure the humans remained submissive after the war.

Vampires had spent far too much time hiding and lurking in the shadows, frightened of the mob mentality of humans. It was where the myth came from that vampires couldn't walk about in the day. It was wrong, they *could* move about in the day, they had merely preferred to hunt at night when there were fewer people, and those who were around were usually easier prey.

But as the vampire numbers increased, so had their compulsion to be free of the shadows. He helped his father lead the attack, taking them all into battle and securing the world for their own means. The war was time-consuming and brutal, but in the end, they emerged the victors, and Braith had every intention of making sure it stayed that way.

He wasn't going back to the shadows, and he wasn't going to let the inferior humans relegate him to such a role again. No matter how much she believed in her words.

Although, most humans had little fight left in them. They were too frightened and beat down to offer much resistance to the vampire rule. Except for a group of humans who hid in the woods, plotting against them, and causing more death and trouble to his kind than Braith would have liked. A group he now knew this girl was a part of.

A kernel of anger curled through him as he studied her. She represented everything he'd fought against, everything he hated so much, yet he held the hands clinging so fervently to him. She seemed to realize her grasp on him as a look of shame crossed her face moments before she released his hand.

"I see," he said.

She didn't speak again but turned away, her head bowing. She tried to stifle a yawn, but the dark shadows under her eyes belied her attempt to hide her exhaustion from him.

"I will show you to your room," he said.

Her head snapped up; her eyes darted rapidly around the room. He sensed her urge to flee, but they both knew there was nowhere for her to go.

"*My* room?" she croaked.

"Unless you would prefer to spend the night with me."

Her mouth dropped as her gaze snapped back to his. He could hear the frantic beat of her heart pounding crazily in her chest as she made a small sound of alarm. "No!"

Braith found himself a little insulted by her vehement cry. He was many things, but he wasn't as hideous as she appeared to believe. He quirked an eyebrow at her and wondered to himself how this frail slip of a girl could cause such a strange reaction within him.

She was nothing special, nor was she the type of woman he preferred. His usual type was curvy, graceful, beautiful, and *eager*. This girl was challenging, pointy, skinny, and anything but eager as she gazed at him in disgust.

"I didn't think so," he murmured.

He rose abruptly and strode across the room to stand in the

43

doorway of the side apartment. He turned back to her. She had risen but remained unmoving by the sofa with her hands folded before her.

The daylight filtering through the windows turned her hair the color of a dark flame. The subtle light was kind to her sharp angles, making her appear prettier. He soaked in the splendor of her. She may not be beautiful, but she was the most magnificent thing he'd seen in years.

CHAPTER FIVE

"IT'S A SHOWER."

Aria jumped in surprise, spinning at the sound of the purred words. The prince was leaning casually in the doorway of the bathroom, his arms folded over his broad chest. Though his customary glasses were in place, she could feel it as his eyes rapidly scanned her.

When she stepped back, her heel connected with the cold bottom of the contraption he labeled a shower. It was different than the massive tub in his room as it was a small stall with a distorted glass door making it impossible to see through it.

He strode toward her, his large body powerful and graceful as he moved with the eerie agility inherent to his kind. Aria tilted her head back as she gazed at him in silent awe. She hadn't seen him since last night, but she realized she hadn't imagined his size, his air of authority, or his rugged masculine beauty. In fact, it seemed even stronger and more overbearing today than yesterday.

He stopped before her, placing his hand on the wall beside her head as he reached around her with the other. Despite herself, a strange tingling gripped her body. She instinctively leaned closer to him, inhaling his masculine scent of spices, earth, and something more potent.

Something feral and primitive, she realized.

It should have scared her away, but she found herself fighting the strange urge to move closer, to touch him, to allow his scent to cover her completely. Her traitorous fingers twitched with the sudden urge to feel him.

Aria jumped in surprise, moving away from the strange contraption as water suddenly sprayed out of the faucet, wetting the back of her bare legs. She turned, incredulity filling her as she stared at the water shooting from the nozzle above. The prince turned the two handles below it, gradually adjusting the flow and heat of the water.

"Amazing," she whispered.

"I suppose it is."

She jolted when she felt his hand within her hair, stroking tenderly over it. She turned toward him, unable to speak as he wrapped it leisurely around his finger. She couldn't move away from him, couldn't reach up to tug her hair back. She could only stand in surprise as he coiled it halfway around his finger before lifting his gaze to her again.

"You will enjoy it, Arianna."

For a moment she had no idea if he meant it was him she would enjoy, or if it was the shower. And she wasn't sure either, as all she craved was to know what his mouth felt like.

Ugh, she was losing her mind; captivity was doing strange things to her. *Enemy*, she reminded herself fiercely. He is the *enemy*, but he didn't feel like her enemy right now.

Then, his finger unraveled from her hair and he took a small step back. "I have sent for someone to assist you again."

She was perfectly capable of taking care of herself. "That's not necessary."

"You are my guest, and as such, you will be afforded the luxuries of a guest."

She quirked an eyebrow as she studied him. "I'm a *guest* now, am I?"

"You are whatever I choose for you to be," he growled back. "For *however* long I choose for you to be."

Despite the heat of the water at her back, Aria felt a chill race down her spine. Every warm feeling she'd been experiencing washed out of her as she was slapped in the face with the cold reality of her life. No matter how good he smelled, she shouldn't have forgotten that, not even for a minute.

She was an idiot.

The thin gown they placed out for her to sleep in last night was beginning to cling to her body from the steam rapidly filling the room. Her heel connected with the bottom of the shower again as he leaned closer to her.

He was near enough she could see the dark bristles of hair lining his firm jaw. Close enough she could see the sharp tip of his canines as his lips skinned back in a tight-lipped smile. Canines she knew could pierce her skin and drain her in the blink of an eye.

"Being a guest isn't such a bad thing, Arianna, now is it?" he murmured.

He was playing with her like a cat with a mouse. She knew it, but to her dismay, she was ashamed to realize she couldn't shake this strange, horrific, attraction toward the vile creature.

She shook her head, trying to rid herself of the tangled coil of emotions wrapping around her, but she could only stare wordlessly at him as he continued to lean over her, his hand resting centimeters from her head. The thick muscles of his biceps flexed, and though she couldn't see his eyes, she was sure his gaze was focused on her mouth.

The tentative clearing of a throat brought both of their gazes to Maggie. She stood in the doorway, her large brown eyes questioning as she glanced at the two of them. In her arms, she clutched a couple of towels, a few bottles of something Aria didn't recognize, and what appeared to be fresh clothes.

She was glad it was Maggie and not Lauren or Julia, but she didn't like the idea of someone seeing her naked, or helping her dress again.

The prince stared silently at Maggie for a moment before stepping away. He strode forward, pausing briefly at Maggie's side to gaze upon the things gathered within her arms.

"No heels," he commanded gruffly. "And *no* perfume or anything floral scented."

Maggie started, her gaze darted to the things within her arms before returning to the prince. Her forehead furrowed, her dark eyebrows drew together as she stared quizzically at him. Aria didn't understand the woman's strange reaction to the prince's words.

Perhaps Aria was the only one who didn't wear the awful monstrosities that passed as shoes around here. But even as she thought it, she knew she was wrong. Maggie was wearing simple, comfortable looking shoes, so why did the woman look so confused by his words?

Maggie shook her head as if to clear it, her forehead relaxed. The prince was gone by the time Maggie picked the heels up from the pile and dropped them on the floor. She turned her attention to Aria, who was too tired and confused to offer any protest as she was once again scrubbed, cleaned, and dressed in another article of clothing she never would have considered wearing before.

The silky green dress floated about her ankles as she moved and seemed impractical to her. Her feet remained blessedly bare.

She walked silently behind Maggie as they slipped through

the luxurious room she had spent last night in, then the small sitting room before it, and finally back into the main room.

The prince was standing before one of the bay windows, looking down at the gardens. His hands were folded behind his back as he rocked leisurely on his heels. He didn't look at them but gestured toward the door. Maggie bowed her head, nodded to Aria, and slipped away.

"I had some food brought up for you," he said.

Aria had already noticed the heaping mounds of food piled on the tray in the middle of the room. Her mouth watered as her stomach rumbled loudly. She'd never seen so many fantastic looking things in her life.

She remained frozen, uncertain of what to do as she gazed at the cheese, fruits, breads, and meats on the tray. It was enough to feed the people within the caves for a day, as they all scarcely ate, and survived on little. Aria couldn't remember a day when she hadn't gone to sleep at least a little hungry.

This night might be her first.

"Arianna?"

She turned toward the prince, blinking rapidly as her stomach rumbled so loudly, she was embarrassingly sure he heard it. He stared at her for a moment; his eyebrow quirked over the dark lenses of his glasses.

"You are hungry, Arianna, you must eat."

She nodded, but she couldn't bring herself to step up to the overflowing tray, not when so many others would go hungry today. Not when her *family* would go hungry today. It didn't seem right.

For the first time, she allowed herself to think about her family. It hurt too much to think about them before, and exhaustion had blessedly dragged her rapidly under last night, but now they filled her thoughts.

Her family would be worried sick about her, half-crazed with their loss and their torment over her new situation. Poor William was probably devastated. Her father and Daniel would stoically move onward, burying their misery, which would only eat them alive inside, as it always did. They would immerse themselves in plans, future attacks, and their resentment and hatred for the vampires would fester until it consumed them, as it had destroyed so many others.

Aria shuddered; she wrapped her arms around herself. She stared at the prince, but she couldn't see him through the waves of homesickness swamping her. And then there was Max. Poor Maxwell, trapped somewhere within this town, with some creature Aria highly doubted was being as kind to him as the prince was to her.

She didn't like to think about what that monster was doing to strong, caring Max. Now that she'd opened the can of worms, she couldn't get it to close again. She wasn't the most experienced person in the world, but she had lived on the far edges of society long enough to know the cruelty committed by vampires and by corrupt people.

Her family tried to shelter her, but there were some things they could never protect her from. Max would be experiencing many of those things over his time with that woman.

The faint touch on her arm caused her to jump. Her hands fisted as she instinctively sought to fight off her offender, but she managed to catch herself before she launched a punch at the prince.

She expected his kindness would vanish if such a thing happened, and though she'd never expected to live long, she didn't have a death wish. She blinked the prince into focus, struggling not to let him see how lost and alone she felt right now.

"I wasn't thinking last night, Arianna; I'm not used to having humans around for more than an hour or two. You have to eat; I know you are hungry."

Her traitorous stomach rumbled again in enthusiastic response to his words. She almost refused the food, but denying something that might aid her, in the end, was foolish. His frown deepened; his concern became apparent.

"Come," he said.

He led her to one of the sofas and settled her on it before turning to the tray. Aria watched as he filled a plate with food. She was confident he'd never done this for anyone; she couldn't understand why he was doing it for her, or why he rescued her from the ugly little vampire of yesterday.

She wondered if he'd ever reveal his reason for claiming her, she doubted it. He turned back to her and handed her the overflowing plate. There were foods on it she didn't even recognize.

She stared at it before he handed her a napkin and a fork. She twisted the fork in her hand as she inspected it. She'd seen them before, had used them a few times, but she wasn't well versed in the art of using a utensil. She much preferred her fingers, but she suspected the use of fingers wouldn't be overly accepted here.

He placed a smaller tray over her lap, and then took the plate back to set the plate on the tray. Aria's hands trembled as she moved the fork awkwardly in her grasp. She stabbed at some of the fruit before successfully spearing it with the strange utensil.

She itched to dive into the heaping plate of goodies but forced herself to at least try to appear civilized in this grand place. The prince placed a glass of some orange colored liquid beside her.

"What is that?" Aria inquired, heat coloring her face as she realized she'd forgotten to swallow her food before she spoke.

He didn't acknowledge her breach in manners as he sat on the sofa beside her. "Orange juice, I've heard it's rather tasty. Humans seem to like it anyway. We grow the trees within the gardens and greenhouses."

Aria lifted the glass, sniffed suspiciously at it, and then

cautiously took a sip. The liquid was cool, sweet, and refreshing. She downed the rest of the glass in one swallow.

"You approve?" he asked.

She smiled tremulously at him as he leaned over to refill her glass. She studied him questioningly; she was unable to understand why he was doing this for her, why he was so kind to a rebel human. She didn't dare ask him; she didn't think he would appreciate her mentioning it. Instead, she decided to enjoy her delicious meal.

She dug in with renewed enthusiasm, somewhere along the way she even forgot he was watching her as she repeatedly helped herself to more of the delicious concoctions on the tray. Her stomach was bloated but full for the first time when she finally pushed her plate aside, wiped her mouth with her napkin, and sighed contentedly.

"Are you full now?" His voice was tinged with amusement; a half smile curled his upper lip as he watched her.

Aria ducked her head; heat flooded her face as she realized what she must have looked like in front of him. She'd eaten almost half of the copious amounts of food on the tray. She'd consumed more than she usually would have in three days.

"Yes," she admitted.

"Good. I must go out for a bit, but if there is anything you require Maggie has been instructed to get it for you. You only have to ring for her. There is also a guard stationed outside your door, don't consider escape."

Aria recoiled; she struggled to keep her face impassive, and her outrage hidden, as she was starkly reminded she was a prisoner in this place. She would never be free again unless she did something to try and change her circumstances.

He'd been kind to her so far, but how long could she expect that to last? Aria folded her hands in her lap. She tried to keep her terror hidden from him, but she knew he could sense it.

"I won't be gone long."

Aria managed a small nod. It was all she could do to make that gesture; she didn't trust herself to speak. The prince rose, straightened the dark shirt he wore, and reached for the cane propped against the couch.

She saw the head of the cane was a silver wolf seconds before his large hand closed around it. She didn't know why he used the thing; he didn't limp or struggle with moving. Perhaps he thought it made him appear more dignified, or it was a weapon of some sort.

He was dressed more sharply than yesterday and sporting the ring marking him as the prince of the house of Valdhai. That marked him as a member of the family who ruled the vampires, and the world, for the past hundred years. He wasn't wearing it yesterday. Whatever he had to do today, it appeared it was relatively significant, and official.

The wolf rose beside him; its green eyes were bright as it stared at Aria for a full minute before turning its attention back to its master. The prince whistled for the wolf, who padded eagerly over to him before they both slipped out the door.

Aria remained sitting after the sound of the lock slid closed with a note of finality that frightened her.

It took her a moment to gather her thoughts, but once she did, she launched to her feet and scurried through the apartment. He'd left her alone to search through things; left her to try and uncover a weapon.

Silly, silly vampire, Aria thought as she scoured through the rooms. But the more she searched, the more she realized that perhaps he hadn't been so foolish. There was nothing she could use to defend herself with.

She moved through the library, and then another small sitting room that was apparently his. Hesitating, she stopped at the edge of his bedroom. She knew it was his by the dark, wood framed bed with a thick red blanket and mound of pillows.

The furniture was masculine, and though she didn't know what a lot of it was, she discovered some things held his clothes. His scent hung heavily in the room and on the clothing. She inhaled deeply, savoring his smell even as she looked for something to destroy him with.

Yep, she'd officially lost it, and she didn't think she'd get it back until she was free of this place.

Turning away from the clothes, her gaze lingered on the massive bed. A strange tingling sensation worked its way through her belly. It heated her from the inside out as she was suddenly swamped with the longing to see him again, to hear his voice, to breathe in his untamed scent.

Instead of continuing her search, she found herself retreating from the room and the unfamiliar wave of heat spreading through her. She'd never fled from anything in her life, and now she was running from a smell and *feelings*?

She hadn't been too afraid to risk becoming a blood slave, but the sight of his room was enough to turn her into a total coward. It was complete insanity, and yet she couldn't stop her feet from insistently moving away.

Her head spun, she couldn't get to her room fast enough. She leaned against the door, breathing heavily as her body trembled. She was beginning to hate herself, and yet even that emotion wasn't strong enough to outweigh the growing yearning curling through her. Aria didn't know what she was yearning for, but she knew it had to do with him, and she didn't like it.

Her fingers shook as she forced herself away from the door and back to the task that sent her into his room in the first place. She had briefly searched the room she was given last night, but even so, she went through it again. She'd been exhausted and barely able to stay awake when she was brought in here. It was entirely possible she missed something.

Her attention focused on the antique looking nightstand beside the bed she slept on last night. It was far different from the hard floor of the caves and forest she was used to; even the pallets of straw she sometimes slept on had nothing on the softness of the bed.

The bed, she decided as she studied the thick mattress and spongy pillows, was almost as good as the shower, but not quite. She tried not to think of her family and their conditions right now as she grabbed the wooden stand and tipped it over. Tried not to think of the hunger and discomfort they were going through as her gaze fell to the legs of the stand.

She knelt before it and sat back on her heels as she studied the spindly pieces of wood. It wouldn't be the best stake, that much was obvious, but it was better than nothing, and nothing was all the other rooms had to offer her.

Leaning forward, she grabbed one of the legs and snapped it free. The wood was ragged, thin; she would only get one chance to use it before it broke. She'd only get one chance before he snapped her neck in retaliation anyway.

Although she knew the possibility of escaping was slim, she would have to make sure it was a damn good chance if she had any shot at surviving and making a break for it. It would be a major boost to the resistance if she somehow, miraculously, managed to destroy the prince. She ignored the twisting guilt in her stomach at the thought of killing Braith. It had no place here.

Rising to her feet, Aria hurried from the room. She grabbed the knife she'd been given to cut her meat with, and four books from the library. She made sure to pull the books from different shelves and carefully rearranged the other ones to hide the holes.

Returning to her room, she used the books to prop the stand

back up and made sure nothing of the books showed from every angle of the room.

Retreating to the bathroom, she leaned over the toilet as she hastily sharpened the slender piece of wood with the knife. The toilet was another contraption she was beginning to appreciate, especially now. A sense of urgency filled her; she needed to get the knife back before he returned. She didn't think he would notice the missing books, there were so many of them after all, but the knife would most certainly be missed.

Shavings fell into the toilet as she carved the end of the wood into a deadly tip. It took several flushes before all the shavings disappeared. Raising the stake, she examined her handy work with an appreciative eye. It wasn't much, she would have preferred her bow and arrows, but if given the right opportunity, it would work.

Aria didn't know what she would do if somehow, miraculously, she managed to take down the prince, but that was a problem she would face when it occurred. Until then, she was happy to have some weapon. It emboldened her and gave her a sense of confidence she'd lacked since entering the palace.

She stood before the mirror, carefully positioning the stake in between her breasts. The cumbersome undergarments they heaped on her came in handy as she adjusted the dress to conceal the thin stake.

Her eyes were wild as she studied her reflection in the bathroom mirror. She had to regain control of herself, but she was terrified of what he would do to her if he somehow found the stake.

He'd kill her, she was sure of it. She was also certain if she didn't make some attempt to escape she'd die anyway. At least, if she were successful, she might help the rebellion by taking down one of the more powerful vampires with her.

CHAPTER SIX

THE NEXT FEW days passed in much the same way. Aria would stash her weapon under her mattress before Maggie arrived in the morning to assist her in dressing. Aria refused Maggie's help with the shower though; she had it figured out now.

She even had the razor and shaving part of it mostly down and didn't slice herself nearly as much as in the beginning. She still wasn't any good with the zippers or buttons of the dresses, and because of that, she was grateful for Maggie's help.

After Maggie left, she would slip the stake back into her dress, reassured by the solid press of it against her flesh as she bided her time and awaited the right opportunity.

The prince sat with her at breakfast every morning and then disappeared for a few hours during the day. In his absence, Aria would wander around aimlessly, growing increasingly anxious and frustrated with her captivity.

Around noon another heaping tray of food would be sent up, she would eat it alone, and miserable. The prince would return, talk with her for a bit, sit with her while she ate dinner, and retire to his room.

It was the loneliest Aria had ever been, and she'd spent many days and nights alone in the woods, or within the caves. But on those occasions, she'd always known she would return to her friends and family and their loving company. Now, she had little hope of that, and the rest of her days may consist of being confined to these rooms.

It would only be a matter of time before she went crazy from it.

Aria meandered into the library again. She studied the walls of books, her gaze roaming over the thick leather bindings. She often found herself in this room, curious as to what the books contained within their covers, speculating about the stories within them. She moved toward them unhurriedly and trailed her fingers over their spines. The leather was cold, smooth, and unyielding beneath her fingertips. She yearned to know what they said.

Oh, she knew a few words, not many, but enough to decipher plans and most of a message, but that didn't help her with these hardbound mysteries. She could make out most of the titles, but when she opened the covers, she found almost everything inside blurred into gibberish. It frustrated her to have them so close by, mocking her inability to read and understand them.

She slipped one of the books free from the others. It fascinated her most for some reason. Opening it, she leisurely flipped through the somewhat yellowed pages as she picked out the words she recognized.

Shaking her head, Aria sighed as she closed the book and slid it back onto the shelf.

"Something against *Ivanhoe*?"

Aria nearly shrieked as her head snapped up. She hadn't heard the prince enter the apartment, but there he was, leaning against the doorway with his head bowed as he studied her from behind his glasses. She gulped, unsure of how he would react to finding her here, and confused as to who or what an *Ivanhoe* was.

"*Ivanhoe?*" she croaked.

He remained unmoving; his brow creased thoughtfully. "Yes, Sir Walter Scott's tale of *Ivanhoe*. It's quite entertaining, and something you would probably enjoy as he was a bit of a rebel himself."

Aria couldn't help but smile at the teasing tone of his voice. Though she was lonely and lost here, she found his company oddly comforting. Probably because he was one of the only two people she had to talk to in this strange, uncertain world.

"Oh," Aria glanced back at the novel, glad to finally know what the title of it was. "I see."

He moved away from the door and strolled toward her. Stopping beside her, his arm brushed against hers as he stretched around her to retrieve the book she had just replaced. Aria's heartbeat picked up, her skin prickled and warmed at his nearness. Even as she cursed her traitorous body, her toes curled.

She didn't trust him and still despised his kind, but he'd been nothing but pleasant to her over the past few days. The more time she spent here, the more fascinated she became with him. She hated that feeling, but she couldn't shake it. She thought it must have something to do with the fact she was trapped here and dependent on him.

Seeming to sense her strange reaction to him, he froze with his arm pressed against her chest as he inhaled deeply. The prince didn't require air to breathe, she knew. Right now, he merely savored her scent. That realization only increased the growing heat of her body. She couldn't look at him as he broke the tension by pulling the book from the shelf and held it out to her.

"It was one of my favorites when I was younger. I think you will enjoy it," he said.

Aria stared at the fascinating book. Her fingers trembled when she took it from him, unwilling to admit she didn't know how to read. He already thought her ill-mannered, unkempt, and possibly a little backward. She didn't want him to think she was stupid too because she most certainly wasn't.

"I'm sure I will," she muttered.

His finger was gentle beneath her chin as he nudged it up. "Arianna, do you know how to read?"

Her gaze darted around; she looked everywhere but at him. She couldn't bring herself meet his gaze as she tried to figure out how to answer.

"Arianna?"

She recognized the annoyance tinging his voice as he became aggravated with her. It didn't often happen, usually only when she didn't eat as much as he liked her to, or when she tried to get out of having Maggie help her.

For the most part, he was patient, considerate even, and she found herself liking him almost as much as she hated him for it. Because she was confident something terrible was coming, and he would turn on her. She was convinced this strange kindness was a charade to earn her trust before annihilating her.

"A little," she admitted on a whisper.

If he laughed at her, if he so much as smirked at her, she swore she'd hit him, or stake him, and damn the consequences.

To his credit, he did neither of those things. His finger momentarily stroked her chin before he released her.

"We will have to remedy that," he said. "Come."

Aria stared at his retreating back before he disappeared. Remedy that? What did that mean?

Aria followed him to the sitting room, but he didn't go to the sofa. Instead, he crossed to the seat by the bay window and settled on it. She hesitated, uncertain what to do or say.

His eyebrows rose over the dark lenses as he patted the seat beside him. "I will not bite you, Arianna."

Displeasure filled her as she glared at him, not at all appreciative of his teasing words. She'd never backed down from a challenge before, and she wasn't about to start now. She threw her shoulders back and stalked toward him.

His hand left the seat beside him, sliding away as she awkwardly settled in next to him. He considered her for a moment before taking the book from her, opening it, and placing it on their laps.

Aria gazed at the page, her discomfort growing as she stared at it. The words and letters swam before her on the page, blurring together before snapping back into focus; they still made no sense.

"It's okay," he assured her.

She turned toward him as trepidation trickled through her. The force of his shaded stare burned straight into her soul. His hand wrapped smoothly around her wrist; her breath hitched in her chest, and her heart fluttered like a caged bird.

For a moment, she could only stare helplessly at him, confused by the strange sensations and emotions he aroused in her. Why was he toying with her like this? Why was he so kind when they both knew he would destroy her?

Deciding not to fight against it and play along with his games, she settled back in the seat. Perhaps it was best if he thought she trusted him, that she wasn't waiting for him to rip her throat out. It could work to her benefit, perhaps give her the opportunity to escape she so desperately sought.

He slipped his arm around her waist and pulled her closer to his side. His skin was cool to the touch, not as warm as hers, but not unpleasant either. She found she fit perfectly against him and didn't mind the feel of his cooler flesh; in fact, she almost welcomed it against her heated skin.

She was willing to play the game, but this was so very intimate and cozy. It was something she'd never experienced before; it was unnerving and exciting all at once. She worried she could be lost within his game, swallowed up and destroyed by it. She didn't know the rules as he did, and she had no experience playing it.

She forcefully reminded herself he was a monster, that he was toying with her and taking joy in her discomfort, even if he didn't appear to be. Her fingers twitched as she studied those dark glasses.

Not for the first time, she hoped he would take them off so she could see his eyes; she was desperate to know what color they were. But in the week she'd been here, she never once saw him without those shades.

For one, heart-stopping moment, she thought he would kiss her as he leaned forward a little. She wanted to pull away; she wanted to move closer. Instead, she found herself as caught up as a fly within a spider's web. And what a web it was, she realized as he broke the moment by leaning away from her.

He settled the book more firmly between them. Aria found herself forgetting everything else as his fingers lingered on her waist. Drawing her legs up beneath her, she focused on the secrets hidden within the pages.

She was eager to absorb what he would teach her, and she'd been contemplating the contents of this book for nearly a week now.

Leaning against his side, she followed along as he leisurely read the novel, pronouncing each word carefully as he urged her to sound them out with him. The smile on his face surprised her; it was rare to see such a thing on him. He was always somewhat reserved and perfunctory, but he seemed to enjoy the book as much as she did.

Aria took pleasure in his smile and interjected at times with the few words she knew. She found herself smiling at him as he taught her to read with an endless patience she was troubled to realize she found endearing.

CHAPTER SEVEN

BRAITH OBSERVED Arianna as she sat on the window seat. Her long legs were curled up beneath her; her dark hair was aglow in the daylight filtering through the windows. Though the book was in her lap, she wasn't looking at it. Instead, her hands were pressed against the glass, her nose nearly touching the pane as she stared outside.

It was only then he realized what these past two weeks must have been like for her. She was used to being free, running wild, and being outdoors. This was probably the most time she'd ever spent indoors, perhaps the most time she'd ever spent with a roof over her head and a steady supply of food on her plate.

Food, which he was pleased to notice, that was already putting weight on her. The weight had rounded out her pointed edges; her collarbone didn't stick out as much, her ribs and spine weren't as visible beneath the dresses she wore. Her face had filled out, and her cheekbones weren't so sharp anymore.

She appeared more youthful now; something he wasn't sure was a good thing. Innocence radiated from her, but when she was thinner, she'd looked worldlier and slightly harsher. He found it easier to be indifferent to her then, but not so much now, especially when she stared out the window with that look on her face.

He moved slowly toward her and touched her shoulder lightly. She tensed briefly, but didn't jump away, recoil, or stiffen as she had when she first arrived here. Her doe eyes were brilliantly blue as she stared at him.

He found it difficult to believe he hadn't seen her as beautiful when she first arrived. Yes, she'd been bedraggled, defiant, smelly, and far too thin, but her spirit had been there. Her splendid inner glow always resided within her, and it was one of the most exquisite things he'd ever encountered. He was too astonished by the sight of her to have noticed it. He couldn't help but see it now, just as he couldn't help but see her desire to be free.

"Would you like to go for a walk in the gardens?" he asked.

Hope sprang forth in her eyes, her mouth parted as joy radiated from her. It was such a small thing he offered her, and yet she reacted as if he handed her the world.

"Can I?" she inquired eagerly.

He nodded as his gaze darted to the brightly colored world beyond the window. It had been a while since he enjoyed a walk in the gardens himself, he found he looked forward to it.

"Yes, I'll take you."

She jumped to her feet, and her full lips curved into a grin that bewildered him. She rarely smiled, and when she did, it was never as lovely as this.

"That would be great!" she gushed.

He tried to gather his scattered thoughts as she beamed at him. "Come along then."

Keegan rose and yawned as he roused from his nap. Braith rested his hand on the wolf's head and reassuringly rubbed his fur. Arianna nearly skipped as she hurried forward. She wouldn't remain so happy for long, of that he was confident; unfortunately, it couldn't be prevented.

Walking over to a closet beside the door, he reached in and removed the chain from inside. "Arianna, you must wear this."

Her head tilted to the side as he lifted the thin chain before her. It hung between them, dangling to the ground in a four-foot long pool of gold. She frowned at it, unable to understand what it was he held.

"All blood slaves must wear them in public," he explained, hating the words as he uttered them.

"What is it?"

He didn't like doing this to her; he despised the idea of binding such a free spirit. But it was the rules, and the rules must be obeyed, especially between them. There were already rumors about the two of them drifting through the palace. Whispers about the first blood slave he'd ever kept, gossip about what went on between them, and why he decided to save her, of all people.

It was gossip he didn't plan to answer, but he couldn't allow it to grow more by allowing her to leave this room without wearing the chain. Any hint of caring between a master and their blood slave was strictly forbidden as was any caring between a vampire and a human.

If they suspected he might be developing feelings for Arianna, they would take her from him, and they would kill her. His role as prince wouldn't stop them.

He couldn't let that happen. He may not care for her, but he also didn't plan to see her destroyed in the brutal way they would do it. It wasn't fair to her, and he wasn't willing to let the light she brought to his life go. Not yet anyway, not until he knew what it all meant.

"It's a leash, to keep you bound to me," he explained.

Her brow furrowed as she gave a confused shake of her head. "I don't understand. Leashes are for..."

Her gaze darted to Keegan; understanding filled her eyes before they narrowed. Keegan didn't wear a leash.

"I see," she grated.

"If you are to go out in public you must wear this; it is our custom."

"I've heard rumors of the blood chain," she muttered. "But I thought they were just that, rumors."

If her jaw clenched any tighter, he was certain she would crack her teeth. Her hands fisted at her sides. She radiated rage, but beneath it, he could sense her unhappiness and feelings of betrayal.

She turned toward the window, and her shoulders slumped. He hated the crushing sense of defeat he detected, but even if she couldn't see it, this was best for both of them.

"Okay." Her voice hitched, but her need to go outside outweighed her pride. "I'll wear it."

He wasn't going to remind her she didn't have a choice; she looked defeated enough. She eyed the gold chain as if it were a poisonous snake she was considering decapitating. They were meant to be worn around the neck, or the wrist, depending on what the owner preferred, but he couldn't add to her degradation by placing it around her neck.

He took her hand, slipped it around her wrist and tightened it tenderly. He was the only one who could remove it now that he'd placed it on her. The one who owned and controlled her; everyone would know she belonged to him. He wasn't entirely sure how he felt about that, he didn't like owning her. He did, however, like everyone knowing she belonged to him, and they couldn't touch her. Ever.

She lifted her head and met his gaze. Her upset air vanished as she tilted her chin higher. She may be humiliated, and under his control, but she wasn't going to allow herself to be beaten down.

For the first time, he admitted to himself that he admired this wisp of a human. He'd never thought much of their species (they were beneath him after all), never even given them more than a moment's thought, except for when it came to food and pleasure.

But this girl made him question his opinions of the human race and made him wonder if perhaps they were worth a little more. Or at the very least, maybe *she* was.

Holding her hand, he disliked the feel of the chain against her supple skin. For a second, he almost pulled it off her, but the consequences of such an action would be dire.

"Okay then," he murmured regretfully.

He held the chain as he grabbed his cane. Arianna followed him out the door and slowed as she gazed around the hallway. There wasn't as much awe on her face this time, and he sensed a calculating air behind her troubled eyes.

He glanced at her chest, wondering if today might be the day she tried to use the weapon she had stashed there. The leash might have been the straw to break her back.

He had nothing to be concerned about with the stake. She would have no success if she tried to use it against him. He probably should take it from her, but he was curious to see if she would try something against him. Also, it seemed to comfort her as she hadn't been as jumpy since she acquired it.

He found himself hoping she would grow to trust him enough not to try to attack him. He didn't relish the idea of possibly having to kill her.

The cunning look in her eyes reminded him that no matter how entranced he was by her, she was a rebel. Someone who would take any chance they had to escape if the opportunity were to present itself. He couldn't allow that to happen.

He took her down the back stairs, unwilling to risk running into his relatives again. Two of his bodyguards trailed them; their surprise was evident when they saw Arianna emerge, looking far different than when she went in.

He led her down another hallway before arriving at the doors leading out to the gardens. Keegan stopped at the doors before Braith did; he rubbed briefly against his master's legs before sitting. Braith patted his head, thanking his friend for aiding him, even if it wasn't necessary right now. Something Braith was almost sure the wolf was aware of, just as he was aware of his master's desire to keep it hidden.

"Leave us," he ordered the guards.

The men stepped back into the hallway as Braith pushed the doors open. Keegan sprang forth, eager to be outside. Amazement filtered over Aria's features as she gazed over the gardens they entered.

"It's even more beautiful down here," she breathed.

Braith glanced over the gardens. He'd once found them mildly attractive, but that was a long time ago. He enjoyed them far more seeing them through her eyes.

"I've never seen anything like this," she murmured.

She moved with subtle grace down the colorful rows of flowers, hedges, and statues.

"You don't have flowers in the woods?" he inquired, hoping to draw her into a conversation about her home as she rarely said anything about it, and seemed almost fearful whenever it was mentioned.

"Oh, of course, we have flowers," she replied, her face aglow with the admiration suffusing her. Love radiated from her at the mention of her home, and her eyes sparkled in the light. "But nothing such as these." Her hands trailed over the yellow roses before she bent low to inhale their scent. "Beautiful."

"They're roses."

"Roses," she repeated, running her fingers nimbly over the petals. "I love them."

He released the gold chain; he didn't think she was aware of her freedom as she roamed through the garden. In fact, she was so oblivious to it; he feared she might trip over it as she walked toward the lilacs.

He found this woman captivating and utterly unique in this colorful world of flowers, shrubs, and garden statues. She breathed in the lilacs next. Her nose scrunched as she stepped hastily back, shook her head, and wiped her nose.

"Lilacs," he informed her.

"Hmm."

She eyed them before strolling away, apparently not at all pleased by their aroma. He named each flower for her as they continued their tour of the garden. Though she hadn't liked the lilacs, it didn't stop her from pausing to sniff every other flower along the way. Most of them passed her inspection; some did not.

She froze when they made it to the greenhouse area within the gardens. Her eyes widened as another gasp of pleasure escaped her.

"Oh," she breathed, her hands flying to her mouth in delight. "Oh, it's wonderful."

Braith studied the large, ornate fountain. It had been years since he'd seen it, but he never fully appreciated the beauty of the delicate sculpture until seeing it now. The water flowing from it changed colors in the sunlight beating down on the man and woman staring longingly at each other but never touching.

Arianna's steps were hesitant as she approached the fountain. She reached out to touch the ornate basin with trembling fingertips. The tears in her eyes didn't surprise him; he knew it occurred whenever something awed her. It happened when they were reading together, and the story moved her. He didn't think she was aware of the tears most of the time.

A beautiful smile lit her face as she peered into the fountain;

she laughed when she spotted the fish swimming in the shallow pool. It was the first time he'd heard her laugh, and he had to admit it was a beautiful, refreshing sound. One he enjoyed.

She sat on the edge of the fountain and held her hair back as she watched the fish darting around. Her fingers trailed over the water as she traced their movements. He moved closer to her, picked the leash up and placed it on the fountain beside her.

He didn't think she would try to escape, but if she did, she wouldn't be able to get far with the chain on her wrist. The chain was designed for him and him alone, and he would always be able to find it. No matter how far she got.

"They're beautiful," she said.

He peered into the clear water, momentarily admiring the brilliant colors of the dozens of fish before turning his attention back to her. He found her much more interesting to watch. When she released it, her hair fell about her in dark red waves that glimmered in the sun's rays flowing through the fruit trees surrounding them.

Keegan lifted his head from his paws; his ears perked up as he watched her stand and stroll away from the fountain. She stopped suddenly, tilting her head back and closing her eyes as she absorbed the rays of the sun.

To Braith's utter surprise, and delight, she threw her arms out and laughed as she twirled around in circles, basking in the sunshine.

He couldn't tear his eyes from her; it took everything he had not to grab her and kiss her. He craved so badly to know what that luscious mouth would taste like, what her body would feel like against his, but he wouldn't interrupt this moment for her with his selfish wants.

If he touched her, her joy would vanish. For the first time, he understood the fountain statues and the yearning on their faces.

He was starting to realize that to always look, but never be able to touch, was a particular kind of torment.

What kind of hell had he gotten himself into with her?

ARIA STOOD UNCERTAINLY in the doorway, uncertain as to whether she should enter the sitting room or not. The prince was in there having a quiet conversation with another man; their dark heads bent close together.

She should probably retreat to her room and stay away until this stranger left, but she was curious about this other man. She was also lonely, and her choices were severely limited when it came to company.

Plus, she almost enjoyed the prince's company now, or at least being around him had been fairly pleasant earlier today.

However, she didn't feel like now was the right time to make her presence known. She stepped back, intending to retreat into the shadows when Keegan spotted her and padded over to greet her.

Their attention was drawn to her by the wolf. The prince rose to his feet instantly; his hand seized his cane as he turned toward her. The other man remained seated for a moment, shock evident on his features. Then, he leisurely rose also.

"I'm sorry," Aria apologized.

No matter how well the prince treated her, she was a blood slave; she should know her place, and that was not to interrupt him when he was in the middle of what appeared to be an important conversation. The prince's mouth compressed into a disapproving line; his knuckles turned white on his cane.

"I didn't mean to... I'm sorry," she stammered as she started to retreat.

Instinctively, she knew she'd done something wrong, that her safe position within this household had just been shaken.

"Wait."

It wasn't the prince who spoke, but she froze anyway, her heart raced as the strange vampire studied her keenly. She almost looked to the prince for help, for some sign of reassurance, but she didn't dare let this stranger think she may trust, or like, the prince. No, this was the time to play the role of docile and beaten.

"Come here," the stranger commanded.

Aria's pride pricked, anger shot through her, but she managed to keep her face impassive as she played the role of meek human to the best of her ability. The prince bristled and moved forward; he placed his cane before him as he folded his hands on the handle.

Unsure of the situation she'd placed herself in, Aria hesitated, but she couldn't refuse. Her owner may be a prince, but under blood slave rules she wasn't allowed to disobey any vampire unless they asked things of her only her owner was allowed to take. Such as her blood or her body, and neither of those things was being asked for now.

Swallowing heavily, she clasped her hands before her and strode forward. Though she was often defiant, confident, and bold with the prince, she instinctively sensed those three things had no place here. She kept her eyes downcast, knowing not to look the visitor in the eye as she stopped before them.

The stranger approached her, circling her like she'd seen the packs of wild dogs in the woods circle their prey before attacking. She hoped for strength and patience to help her get through this humiliating, experience. She had to hold her tongue if she was to remain safe.

She chanced a glance at the prince, but he remained mute as he leaned back on his heels. Though he appeared casual, she could see the tension in his shoulders and the tautness of his solid muscles. She didn't know what was going on here, but she sensed it was more than met the eye.

"Not bad brother, not bad."

Aria couldn't stop her head from snapping up as the stranger stopped before her. His hair was the same dark color as the prince's, his features similar, though his nose was somewhat larger and sharper, and his lips thinner. His eyes, unhindered by dark shades, were a deep forest green, and surprisingly beautiful. He was shorter than the prince too, but his shoulders were broader as he stepped closer to her.

Aria had no choice but to move back as he used his height and size to maneuver her. His eyes gleamed with amusement as he pressed closer to her, causing her to retreat another step.

Resentment shot through her, she longed to pull her stake out and drive it straight into his heart. She itched to kill this thing, but revealing her stake now would only earn her certain death. This was not the time to be reckless, not the time to be foolish. If she was ever going to get a chance to escape, she couldn't blow it by losing her temper now.

It didn't matter how much she longed to stand up to this imposing, overbearing, pitiless creature, to do so would only cause problems. Especially since, if his looks and words were any indication, he was a prince in his own right.

Aria had heard rumors there were four brothers and two sisters. She'd also heard there were three brothers and no sisters, or even five brothers and three sisters. The gossip about the royal family swirled outside the palace towns, with the rebel camps knowing even less about them. Aria supposed that was the way the royal family liked it, where no one knew anything about them for sure, and they couldn't be entirely pinned down.

She wondered which of the brothers was older and would one day rule the kingdom. She supposed, in her situation, it didn't make much of a difference.

Her prince remained silent, his indifference causing a small twinge in her chest.

Had she imagined the growing bond between them? Had she chosen to believe he might be starting to like her? What other reason could there be for taking her on a walk today? Why else would he have been teaching her to read? Had she been that gullible?

Of course, she had been, she realized. Utterly exasperated with herself, she forced her head back down. She was nothing to him, she never had been, and never would be. She'd known he was only toying with her, stringing her along to make it hurt more in the end, and though he probably wasn't done playing his game, she was.

Her fingers clenched as she took a deep breath and fought to restrain her temper. She wasn't angry at them, she wasn't even mad at this whole awful situation, but she was *infuriated* with herself.

She was a fool to let her guard down, a fool to think she was anything more than a backwoods, disposable girl to them. Except, she *was* more than that, they just didn't know it.

Her father was a leader, a ruler in his own right. In her world, she was an outstanding hunter and a strong warrior. She didn't have Daniel's knack for making strategies and creating plans, nor did she have William's charismatic ability to rouse people to battle, but she was quick, strong, and highly adept in using multiple weapons.

Yes, she may be a nothing in *this* world, but in her world, she had many different talents and abilities that were greatly admired. In her world, she *was* something; she was loved and respected.

And she missed it fiercely. Heat colored her face; suddenly feeling homesick as she remained expressionless beneath this stranger's cruel perusal of her. She wanted so badly to be free of this room and to take back the last five minutes. She wished she'd never come out here, wished she'd slipped away before either of them noticed her.

This was better, she decided, it was much better this way.

She'd spent the last couple of weeks in a kind of suspended dream. She had been trying to deny reality, but now it was staring her in the face, and it was as grueling and cruel as always. She'd known food, opulence, and cleanliness here, but that was little compared to the respect and unconditional love of her family.

"Perhaps, when you are done with her—"

"I do not think so, Caleb," the prince said forcefully.

Caleb's face twisted into a malicious smile. "You plan on using her until there is nothing left?"

"I have not decided."

Aria shuddered in horror at the words. She forced herself to keep her head down, afraid if she looked at either of them she would start screaming and never stop. She fought the urge to tell them how awful they were, how wrong and horrendous and cruel their world was.

She wanted to scream at them that she didn't deserve this, that her *people* didn't deserve this. She wanted to tell them exactly what she thought of them, but that would only guarantee her death.

She would show them she was more than nothing and something special. To do that she would have to get free of here, she would have to be the first blood slave ever to escape the bonds of their master, and she could do it somehow.

"Leave us," her prince commanded.

Aria glanced up, Caleb was still inspecting her as if she were a side of beef. She hated the leering gleam in his eyes; it reminded her of the creepy little vampire who first claimed her.

"Now!" her prince barked.

The prince had never raised his voice at her. He had been

overbearing and pushy when she first arrived, but he'd never yelled at her. Fresh indignation washed over her, but she buried it beneath her growing fury and sense of betrayal.

She managed a brief nod before turning on her heel; she forced herself not to run as she hurried from the room. She didn't want them to suspect how infuriated she was.

CHAPTER EIGHT

ARIA STAYED MOSTLY in her room for the next few days, she didn't bother the prince, and he didn't bother her. At every meal time, trays of food would be sitting outside the door for her. She took them because not doing so would be foolish.

She planned to attempt an escape, she *would* escape, but to do that she would have to be strong. Food was necessary for that.

The only company she had was Maggie; though the girl was always polite to her, they had little to say to each other, and Aria didn't trust her. On her third day of imposed solitude, the prince came to her room, but she ignored him by pretending to sleep when he opened the door.

On the fourth day, Lauren arrived.

Aria was stepping out of the shower when she spotted the blonde in the bathroom, clothes in hand. Aria froze at the sight of her. Their gazes locked for a poignant moment before Lauren turned and left the room.

It couldn't be a good sign she was here today instead of Maggie. Aria grabbed the towels Lauren left behind, dried herself quickly, and wrapped the towel around her.

She moved warily to the dressing room in between the bathroom and her bedroom. Lauren's hand was resting on the back of the chair as she waited impatiently for her; a cruel smile curved her full mouth as her gaze perused Aria. Aria would have been happy never to see this girl again, and it was more than apparent Lauren felt the same way.

"Where is Maggie?" Aria inquired.

Lauren shrugged absently; she lifted the brush, twisting it within her hand as she eyed Aria maliciously. "I don't know; the prince has requested my services from now on."

Aria's hands clenched. This was just one more way for him to humiliate and put her in her place. He was punishing her for locking herself in her room to hide from him, and he wanted some reaction from her.

She wouldn't give him what he wanted as she vowed to take this punishment without protest. She could take whatever he, and Lauren, threw at her.

She didn't look at the girl as she settled into the chair before her. When Lauren began to brush out her hair, she pulled so sharply at it that she tugged strands of it from Aria's head. Unable to keep herself from wincing, Aria didn't utter a complaint.

Lauren smoothed her hair out, then grabbed some of the barrettes on the table. Revulsion slithered through Aria at the bite marks marring the pale skin of Lauren's wrist and inner arm.

The hateful blonde leaned close to her ear. "The prince was exceptionally hungry this morning."

Aria froze, unable to move or blink as the implication behind those words sank in. No matter what Lauren did to her, no matter what happened within these rooms, it wouldn't do Aria any good to tell the prince about it because Lauren was his mistress, and the one he fed on. He wouldn't believe anything Aria had to say, especially not when it was about the woman who provided for his needs.

Though revulsion filled her, she was ashamed to admit that realization caused an odd twinge of betrayal in her. She detested him; she reminded herself sternly. She wouldn't allow herself to be jealous of his relationship with Lauren because she despised him.

She should be relieved he hadn't turned to her, that he was going to other women, but she wasn't. Why?

She may not understand her strange reaction to these circumstances, but she was beginning to understand Lauren's intense dislike of her. She was threatened by Aria's presence in this place, threatened by whatever it was the prince intended with Aria.

What Aria didn't understand was what *she* was doing here. The prince had someone to sustain and provide for him. Why was she here when he hadn't even once tried to feed on her? Was she merely here for his enjoyment? For him to torment?

She knew the vampires were brutally cruel and indifferent, but this was the first she'd heard of this sort of treatment of a blood slave.

Then again, she'd always assumed a blood slave was drained and tortured physically. Perhaps they were also mentally assaulted and played with until they lost their minds and had to be destroyed because they went stark raving mad.

Aria shuddered at the thought seconds before a barrette jabbed roughly into her scalp. She shot Lauren a dark look, but her protest and irritation died out as she saw the malicious gleam in Lauren's eyes. A sinking feeling filled her as she realized it wasn't only the vampires here who were cruel, but also the humans.

She was completely at Lauren's mercy, a fact driven home by the sharp stab of the next barrette.

Aria withstood it all through the next few days; she took the handfuls of hair she lost in silence. She remained quiet through the skin pinching, jerking, pulling, and shoving it took for Lauren to get her into clothes that fit perfectly once on.

Bruises marred her skin from her chest down, but for some reason, Lauren didn't touch her face. Though she was in pain, Aria wouldn't give Lauren the satisfaction of her tears. She still hadn't seen the prince, but she would be damned if she let Lauren report back to him that she'd been reduced to tears.

Instead, she kept it all inside, letting her resentment fester. She used every abuse to fuel her rage and fan her drive to escape this place. Even when the stake wasn't on her, she always kept it nearby, and there had been a few times she'd resisted the urge to shove it through Lauren's cold heart. She wouldn't waste her opportunity on Lauren though, no matter how much she despised the girl.

She continued to remain hidden away, but if she were going to have a chance to use the stake against the prince, she would have to see him again. She couldn't bring herself to approach him when he was here, and he hadn't returned to her room. She had to stop being such a coward.

Today, she promised herself as she stood beneath the warm water of the shower, hoping to ease the ache of her taut and bruised muscles. Today, she would stop hiding and face him again. Today, she would start playing the game once more. It was the only chance she had of ever regaining her freedom.

She was climbing out of the shower, unaware anyone else was in the room until Lauren shoved her. Her knees smacked off the marble floor which stung her palms and bruised her hip. One of her ribs gave way with a sharp crack as her ribcage connected with the corner of the shower stall.

It was the first time a cry of pain escaped her, but she wouldn't let it keep her down. Gritting her teeth, Aria cradled her bruised side with her hand as she pushed herself up. Gingerly, she rose to her feet and glowered at Lauren.

ERICA STEVENS

She'd been trampled by horses before; it had hurt worse than this, but not by much. At least then she'd rolled under most of the horse's hooves, and it was quick. Now, she was on a constant collision course with the woman torturing her daily.

She didn't know how much more she could tolerate before she snapped and pounded the girl into a bloody mess. Though she was beaten, and now also broken, Aria was confident she could still take the blonde and just as certain she would face immediate death for her actions.

She was beginning to think death might be worth it if it meant getting to a little revenge on Lauren. The only thing holding her back was she planned to exact revenge on *all* of them, not just the bitch before her. She was going to show everyone she was more than the simple-minded, weak blood slave they believed.

Aria held her ribs as she defiantly met Lauren's smug smile. She walked into the dressing room, trying not to cry as Lauren pulled the strings of her dress harshly. She ignored the tray of food outside her door, preferring to curl up in bed as she attempted to fight off the agonizing pain crushing her chest.

It didn't help that she couldn't get the dress off because she couldn't work the horrible ties free. For the first time, she didn't bother to dig the stake out from under the mattress.

Somehow, she wasn't quite sure how, she managed to fall asleep for a little bit. It was dark when she woke again to Lauren's prodding. "Get up, you lazy creature."

Aria bit her bottom lip, drawing blood as she held back a moan. Lauren pulled unapologetically on the ties, finally releasing the snug binds pinching her ribs. Aria sagged in relief, panting in as much air as her abused ribs would allow. Lauren released her and left the room, leaving Aria to figure out how to get the dress over her head and the nightgown on.

It took more strength and energy than she cared to admit to

82

wiggle her way free of the dress. Tomorrow morning, she was going to throw the thing out. It was the piece of clothing she hated most now, even more so than the ridiculous heels.

Sitting on the edge of the bed, she tried to gather her strength to slip the nightgown over her head. She could just leave it off, Lauren hadn't bothered to help her out of the ridiculous undergarments she had to wear here, but she couldn't bring herself to sleep in such a vulnerable state.

It was bad enough having to wear the silly nightgown to sleep when she was used to so much more, but to wear less would be far worse. She was in constant danger here; she must be clothed to be at least a little prepared for that threat.

Drawing in as deep a breath as she could, she knotted the nightgown before her and bit by bit, slipped her arms into the sleeves. She winced as pain shot through her battered ribcage. Struggling not to cry out, she bit her tongue as agony tore through her side.

"Arian..."

Aria froze with her hands were trapped inside the sleeves of the nightgown. She hadn't heard the prince coming. In the forest, she heard a field mouse from a mile away. But here, in this strange and deadly place, where she needed her senses the most, they were failing her miserably.

She didn't turn to face him; she couldn't bring herself to do so. Instead, she remained unmoving and grateful for the impractical, uncomfortable undergarments that at least shielded some of her nudity from his view.

She kept her head turned away from him and held her breath as she waited for him to take his fill of the damage done to her before he left again. She didn't know what brought him here tonight, not when he'd left her alone for so long, nor did she care. She wanted him to absorb whatever he could of her, and go. She had no fight in her at the moment.

"What happened?" he demanded.

Aria clenched her jaw as she pulled the nightgown further up her arms. She ground her teeth against the throbbing of her body. She refused to answer him or let him see she was at all disturbed by his presence.

Suddenly, he was before her. He seized the nightgown as he attempted to pull it away from her. Aria held on, unwilling to relinquish anything to him. However, he was far stronger than her, and he wasn't injured.

In the end, she lost.

She glared at him as her hands fisted impotently in her lap.

"What happened?" he demanded gruffly.

"Like you don't know!" she snapped.

His mouth compressed into a severe line; a muscle twitched in his cheek. "I wouldn't be asking if I knew. What happened?"

Aria refused to cower beneath the weight of his stare. "Your *bitch* happened!"

Disbelief registered on his face; his mouth parted, and she felt his eyes wander over her again. It was far more of her body than any man had ever seen before, but she didn't give him the satisfaction of trying to shield herself. He already thought her far weaker than him; she wouldn't support his theory by shrinking from his gaze.

"Are you talking about the girl who was here earlier?" he asked.

Aria didn't appreciate being played with. Especially not right now. She intended to go back to sleep and give her body a chance to heal before it was assaulted again tomorrow.

"Yes, *that* girl," she replied with a sneer.

The prince's gaze traveled over her once more and she could feel the blistering heat of his anger.

"Why did she do this?" he asked.

Aria shrugged then winced as she instantly regretted the

action. She clamped down on the small cry that almost escaped. Inhaling sharply through clenched teeth, it took her a moment to speak again.

"Because she can," Aria said. "I *am* just a blood slave after all."

That muscle in his cheek was throbbing now as his nostrils flared. "You may be a blood slave, but you are *my* blood slave."

Aria refused to meet his gaze; she kept her hands folded in her lap as she focused on the back wall.

"Stand up," he commanded gruffly. Aria didn't move. "Get up!"

The words were practically snarled at her, but she still didn't move. She'd been beaten down enough over the past week, she would take whatever small victories she could get, and disobeying him was one such victory. She didn't think about the fact he could do whatever he fancied to her right now. She didn't care anymore; she would withstand whatever he did to her and anything else they threw at her until she broke free.

He made a low hissing sound, and then his hands were on her arms. She was surprised by how tender his touch was as he lifted her. He set her on her feet; his hands rested on her arms as he stepped back.

Heat flooded her face. At least on the bed, she'd been somewhat hunched over and sheltered from him, but not anymore. She couldn't stop her hands from instinctively fluttering up to try and cover herself, but he pulled them aside.

Aria buried her annoyance and despair as she stood before him with her body almost entirely exposed for him to see. He didn't leer at her, didn't stare at her as if she were inferior to him and unworthy.

His fingers trailed across her ribs, running over the edge of the dark bruise there. Though she kept her face impassive, her body instinctively flinched away from his touch as it neared her broken rib.

His hand stilled on her skin, and his palm flattened on her. "Your rib is broken."

"I know."

He raised his head slowly; she could sense the question behind those dark lenses. She didn't answer it, as far as she was concerned, he didn't have to know how it happened. He already knew who, and why, and that was enough for her.

Instead, she stayed immobile, frozen beneath his touch. His hand remained against her as it cradled the broken bone beneath her skin. His touch was far kinder than she'd expected from him; he was the one who had allowed this to happen after all.

"And she did this to you?" he asked.

Aria remained silent, trying to keep the tears in her eyes back. She didn't want him to see them, didn't want him to know that his gentleness unsettled her more than Lauren's abuse. Lauren's behavior was expected; his was not.

She'd decided he was nothing but evil and she preferred having nothing to do with him. She would kill him if given a chance.

"Arianna?" he prodded.

She turned her head away. "Yes. She did this."

She felt the tension that seized him, yet his hand against her ribs remained gentle. He leaned closer to her, his mouth momentarily pressing against her ear. She could feel the brush of his lips on her skin.

Though she was determined to hate him, her body betrayed her by pressing closer to him. Instinctively, she sought the strength radiating from him as her heart beat a little faster and her skin tingled for more of his touch.

"It won't happen again," he vowed.

A single tear slid free, and a shudder tore through her, neither of which she could hide from him. He wiped the tear away before sweeping her into his arms. Aria gasped, expecting new pain to explode through her, but the way he held her kept it from coming. It was so gentle, so sweet that she could only gaze up at him in surprise.

"Don't," she said.

He didn't respond to her simple word or look at her again as he left the room. Aria tried to squirm against him, tried to feel some irritation, but she was so beat down she couldn't muster much of a protest.

True panic ripped through her when he set her down in the middle of *his* room. She tried to jerk free, but he grasped her wrist and pulled her back.

"You should be watched over. Broken ribs can be dangerous," he said as if this was enough of an explanation for everything happening now.

It wasn't, but she didn't argue. She longed to sleep again if she could.

They stared at each other before he released her wrist. He lifted her smoothly again and placed her on the softest, most fantastic thing she'd ever experienced. It was only after she sank into the mattress that she realized she was in *his* bed. Her hands stroked the thick blanket and silky sheets. It was a little bit of heaven here on earth.

Then, the apprehension kicked in. She was in his *bed*! She tried to sit up, but the pain lancing through her side caused an involuntary groan to escape her. He was beside her, his hands tender on her shoulders as he tried to push her back down. She attempted to strain against him, but there wasn't much fight left in her.

"Rest, Arianna, relax, I won't harm you."

She eyed him warily, unable to believe him. He released a low, regretful sound as he shook his head at her.

"You can't sleep alone tonight; you might puncture a lung. You should be watched over, and since I much prefer my bed, you will be staying here for the night," he said.

She gawked at him. He was going to stay in here, with her? She thought her heart was going to leap out of her chest. "I can tape your ribs for you—"

"It's okay, I'll be fine," she assured him quickly.

It would be a little too intimate if he did such a thing; it was bad enough he expected them to sleep beside each other tonight. Plus, she preferred not to have her ribs taped, especially before going to sleep.

Rolling it up within his grasp, he held the nightgown out to her. "Put your arms up."

She frowned at him before gingerly lifting her arms. She strained to keep her face blank as her body screamed in protest. He studied her before rolling the nightgown over her head with subtle ease.

When he finished, she lowered her arms and relaxed a little. He adjusted the gown, pulling the material down her legs. Heat flooded her face; she ducked her head as his hand brushed her thigh. He quirked an eyebrow at her but refrained from commenting on her reaction to his touch.

"Why didn't you tell me about this?" he asked.

"Why would I?"

Frustration darkened his face; his square jaw clenched. "You are to tell me whenever someone mistreats you."

"Don't like it when your property gets bruised?" she retorted.

She didn't know why she baited him or was being so rude when he'd been nothing but kind to her tonight, but she couldn't stop herself. There was something about him, and this whole situation, that caused a volatile reaction from her.

Apparently, he hadn't known what Lauren was doing to her,

and hadn't condoned the girl's violent actions, but she still couldn't stop the bitterness she felt from surging toward him.

He'd been rude to her when his brother was here, but she couldn't expect him to be kind to her in public, could she? Aria shook her head; she was too tired and too battered to try to wade through the conundrum that was him.

"No, I don't," he replied icily.

She scrutinized him from beneath her lashes. Her question had truly aggravated him. "I didn't mean..." her voice trailed off; she didn't know what to say to him.

"Didn't you?"

Aria shook her head, but there were no more words within her. Mainly because Aria was sure she owed him an apology, and she hated being wrong almost as much as she hated saying sorry. Especially to someone who was her enemy, wasn't he?

"Come on," he said. "You need to rest."

She moved back to lay woodenly on the bed; her fingers dug into the blanket when he put it on her. He didn't lie down beside her but stood up, pulled off his coat, and disappeared into the bathroom she'd used upon first arriving. She listened to the water as he washed before returning.

"You will have to eat tomorrow."

Though it was a command, his voice was nowhere near as gruff as before. She didn't take offense to the order; in fact, she sensed a hint of worry in his tone and demeanor. It warmed her further.

Maybe she was far more bewildered and exhausted than she realized she thought dimly. Especially if Aria was already feeling as if she could trust him again when she had so firmly decided it was the last thing she was ever going to do.

"I will," she said.

She closed her eyes and settled in beneath the thick

comforter. She had never been in someone else's bed before, let alone a man's, but for some reason, this didn't feel wrong.

The mattress sank beneath his weight. Aria didn't open her eyes again, despite her determination to stay vigilant, she was already falling asleep. Strangely secure in the bed of a vampire.

CHAPTER NINE

"Lauren?" Braith asked.

The small blonde rose to her feet, a bright smile lit her pretty features.

"Yes, Your Highness?" Hope sprang over the girl's pretty features as she looked eagerly at him.

Leaning against the doorway, he studied the girl as he fought the antipathy surging through him. Other than the few times she'd arrived to tend to Arianna, he'd seen her only a handful of times before. He may have fed off her in the past, he didn't recall doing so, but her reaction to Arianna's presence here led him to believe he had.

"I'd like to know why you think you have the right to lay your hands on my blood slave, for anything other than to help her in the way I told you to?" he asked.

She looked confused as she frowned at him, but alarm filled her eyes.

"I don't know what you mean," she said.

"Don't play with me," he growled, losing patience with the girl. "I won't hesitate to kill you."

She stepped back and glanced at the door as her fight or flight instinct kicked into gear.

"Now tell me, why did you feel you had the right to damage her?" Braith inquired.

Her mouth opened and closed; he could almost see the wheels in her mind spinning as she tried to think of an answer. "Your Highness, I uh... I uh..."

"Have we encountered each other before you were summoned here?"

Tears bloomed in her eyes as her lower lip trembled. Her reaction gave him the answer to his question. He didn't feel sorry the encounter obviously meant more to her than to him. What he did feel bad about was that Arianna suffered abuse because of his forgetfulness and extreme lack of caring about the girl before him.

Her head fell back as he strolled across the room to stand before her. Fear radiated from her, but beneath it all, he sensed the distress his disregard for her caused.

"Why do you feel you had the right to treat my property poorly?" he grated.

A single tear slid down her face; her lip trembled more. He was indifferent to her obvious distress, her species meant little to him, and she meant even less.

"I am sorry," she whispered.

"Yes, you are. You are not to return here." He grabbed her chin, drawing her attention back to him when her gaze darted to the doorway behind him. He knew Arianna had entered the room because her presence caused it to brighten considerably.

"Don't look at her," he commanded. Apprehension radiated from Lauren as she shook within his grasp. "You are to leave here and never return, if you step foot in this palace again, you forfeit your life."

The color drained from her already pale face as she swayed

unsteadily. Being barred from the palace was a social punishment that would haunt her for the rest of her life. Not only that, but she'd just lost the wages and prestige this job awarded her.

"Do you understand me?" he inquired.

She managed a small nod as she blinked back the tears swarming her eyes. He released her, disgusted by the feel of her skin beneath his hand.

"Get out," he commanded.

The girl scurried away, shooting only a brief, hate-filled glance at Arianna before fleeing his apartment. Braith turned toward Arianna and was surprised by the severe frown marring her features, and the hostility simmering in her eyes.

Was this the same girl he'd woken up to find half sprawled over him with her hair spread across him?

The awkward position had made it difficult to extricate himself without waking her. He'd been half afraid if she woke he wouldn't be able to stop himself from easing the frustration finding her body pressed against his had aroused.

She'd been so peaceful and trusting in her sleep that he'd almost forgotten she could be as prickly as a cactus. It was impossible to forget it now.

"You didn't have to be so cruel to her," she admonished.

"Are you defending the girl?" He had to fight to keep the disbelief from his voice.

Arianna tilted her head. The radiance streaming through the windows accentuated the deep red of her hair. She still wore the nightgown, but in the sunlight, he could see through some areas of it. He didn't think she was aware of the effect the light had on it, if she had been, he was sure she wouldn't be wearing it right now.

Something new rose out of the hopeless pit that had been his soul for so long. Something that had nothing to do with his unfulfilled desire from this morning or his increased craving for her blood.

He didn't know what was going on with this strange girl, why she affected him as she did, but he admitted to himself that whatever she did to him was deep and profound. It was also something he'd never experienced before.

He knew she was special and that she caused a strange reaction in him, but looking at her now, he realized he wasn't going to let her go. He'd been keeping her here, under the delusional assumption he would one day trade her off, but that would *not* happen. He may not be using her in the way a blood slave was supposed to be used, but he wasn't going to allow someone else to use her in that way either.

"I'm not defending her," she murmured. "But you didn't have to be so mean to her. You were the one who forgot about her, and then you brought her here to take care of what she mistook as her replacement. You hurt her."

His eyes narrowed at her. Was she scolding him? Was she really questioning his way of life and the things he did?

She was a child for crying out loud, a *human* child. His hands fisted at his side, he fought the urge to go to her and shake some fear into her because he was beginning to realize she didn't have a healthy enough dose of it for him.

"Am I supposed to care?" he grated.

She blinked in surprise, and her crystalline sapphire eyes darkened in disbelief. Then, she shook her head, and her face went blank. Her hands clasped demurely before her, but he was beginning to realize it was an act. There was nothing demure or weak about this girl; she may play the part well, but there were many layers beneath her docile exterior.

"I suppose not," she responded.

Even her voice had taken on a decorous tone.

"She also harmed you," he reminded her.

Arianna shifted subtly; though she remained outwardly meek, he sensed the raw loathing spiking through her.

"That doesn't make what you just did right. You took her job and her pride away. Two wrongs don't make a right, or at least that's what my dad always told my brothers and me."

Despite his frustration with her, and his growing urge to shake her, her words piqued his interest. It was the most she'd talked about her family since arriving. "How many brothers?"

Her fingers fidgeted with the sleeves of her nightgown. Her gaze was sad and distant as her thoughts turned toward her family. Finally, she didn't look frustrated with him as she had all morning. He found he preferred her animosity to the sorrow engulfing her now.

"Two," she replied. "Anyway, you didn't have to frighten her. She was simply jealous because she thought I was a threat to her when it came to you."

"And why would she think that?"

She rolled her eyes at him as she folded her arms over her chest. He didn't miss the subtle wince of soreness the action caused her.

"I don't know. She was wrong, of course; I mean I'm most certainly not a threat to her or anyone else. Especially when you were feeding on her—"

"I was what?" he interrupted her rush of words.

Arianna fiddled with her nightgown sleeves again, obviously uncomfortable with this topic. "Feeding on her," she said.

"I don't know where you got your information, but it is wrong."

"Oh," she said faintly, her forehead furrowed in consternation. "Oh, I see. I thought..." her voice trailed off. "I must have misunderstood her, or you. I simply assumed the bites on her were from you."

"You think I would forget her that quickly?"

She shrugged, but there was a hint of remorse in the set of her shoulders.

"You think that little of me?" he asked.

She observed him with a keen new interest. "I don't know what to think of you," she admitted. "I really don't. This whole situation..."

She held her hands out before her; her gaze darted over the room before turning back to him. "I don't know what to make of any of it. It's scary, and it's disconcerting, and I'm so far out of my league here that I have no idea what's going on. I don't know if you're playing with me while plotting my death. I don't know if this is the calm before you drain me dry. I don't know what is going on here, and it's tearing me up inside! I've heard the stories, and I've seen the damage your kind can do. I don't know how to play these games; I don't understand the hatred and resentment festering here! How the hell am I supposed to know what to think, or what to do, when I don't even know how much longer I'll be allowed to live?"

Her voice was ragged and filled with raw emotion by the time she stopped speaking. Her shoulders heaved; her eyes were earnest and pleading. For the first time, her façade crumbled, and he saw the terrified, irate girl beneath the timid exterior. She took a ragged breath as her shoulders bowed again. She clasped her hands before her and tried to appear sedate once more, but they both knew she couldn't un-ring that bell.

He began to understand how she felt. She had kept so much of it hidden from him, but now she'd laid it all bare. He'd known something more lay beneath her docile exterior, but he began to see the pride and heart of this trapped, cornered girl.

He felt the stirrings of a new emotion and was surprised to realize it was sympathy. He'd never felt sympathy for anyone before and assumed he'd never be able to experience it or care to.

"Well, anyway, she thought more of what transpired between the two of you," Arianna said.

Braith clenched his fists against the strange feelings within him; feelings that would only make him weak.

"I don't care what she thought." The words were sharper than he intended, but he didn't like that the girl had mentioned such a thing to Arianna, and he didn't like that it bothered him.

Her words also served to remind him of the fact he was hungry. There were a few different women he would visit when the thirst came on him, but he found the idea of feeding on them wasn't appealing at the moment; especially not when he had Arianna standing across from him looking unbelievably striking and smelling delicious.

His veins thrummed with hunger, his hands fisted at his sides. He recalled her words about having to take anything from her by force; he wondered if she still felt the same, or if maybe, just maybe, she would allow him to feed on her.

He didn't think that was likely, not when she still looked at him with distrust most of the time. And not when she believed he tossed women, especially human women, aside like they were nothing. Though, if he were honest with himself, he usually did.

He had tried to be as temperate with her as possible, but after the events of today, he realized it was going to take a lot more to earn her trust, and he realized he wanted her trust more than he wanted the alluring blood flowing through her veins.

The temperature in the room became stifling as he focused on her tempting pulse in her neck. If he was going to get that blood, then he would have to earn her trust.

It was strange to realize he had to work for this; Braith was accustomed to getting whatever he wanted, whenever he wanted. He was used to women throwing themselves at him, not ones continually challenging and refuting him.

She wasn't even quite a woman, not yet anyway. She was

young, and she had known so little in her short life. Yet she was strong-willed, vibrant, and far more willful and captivating than any woman he'd ever known.

"How old are you, Arianna?"

She appeared startled for a moment, then her mouth curved into a smile. "Far younger than you, I'm sure, but I'm seventeen."

He wasn't surprised by the tender age.

"How old are you?" she asked.

"Nine hundred fifty-two."

Her mouth dropped in astonishment. "Wow."

He managed a wan smile. "Yes, wow. I am the oldest of my siblings."

Curiosity lit her features. "How many siblings do you have?"

"Two brothers and two sisters. This is not common knowledge in your world?"

She shook her head. "There is little known about the royal family. It's mostly rumors and innuendo. We don't give much thought to the vampires that have taken so much from us, other than trying to survive from day to day while trying to remain free of your kind."

"I see."

"Do you?"

She met his gaze head-on. It was a trait he admired, even though her stubbornness and inability to look past what he was aggravated him. He decided to let it go for now; continuing to bicker with her wouldn't get either of them anything other than irritated.

"Come here; let me look at your ribs."

He thought she was going to defy him, but she seemed to decide against it as she reluctantly came toward him. He tried not to focus on the subtle glimpses of flesh the light revealed through her nightgown, but he found his gaze repeatedly drawn to her.

She stopped before him, her hands folded in front of her, but at least she didn't pretend to be demure as she gazed haughtily at him. He examined her, admiring that she didn't flinch when he pressed against her broken bone.

"They should be good in a few weeks," he said.

"I know."

His hand lingered on her side, holding her gently for a moment. If he gave her some of his blood she would heal quicker, but he knew she wouldn't take it, and though he was drawn to her more than anyone else he had ever met, he wasn't willing to create the bond between them sharing his blood would produce. He'd never shared his blood before, never mind with a human. It was something he never intended to do, with anyone. Most vampires didn't as it was far too intimate and binding.

Her eyes were bright in the glow of the room as they gradually came toward him. She studied him for a long moment, seemingly trying to puzzle him out. He felt an overwhelming urge to kiss her, to know what she would feel like against him, what she would taste like. To solve at least a little bit of the enigma that was her.

Before he knew what he was doing, he moved toward her. He half expected her to tell him to stop, he gave her the time to do so, but she remained unmoving as his lips brushed against hers.

She stiffened beneath him, her heart lurched violently, and the rapid upswing of her pulse beat against his eardrums. Excitement tore through him, the thirst for her blood gripped him tight as the delicious scent of it assailed his senses.

He struggled to keep his teeth from elongating as the tantalizing urge to bite into her and savor her taste tore through him. He would frighten her if he did such a thing, and that was not what he was looking to do. No, right now all he wanted was to taste her in a different way.

He pulled slightly away from her. He waited for her to shove him back, to tell him to stop, or to leave her alone. It was the last thing he wanted to happen, but he didn't want her to think he was going to force this on her. She observed him circumspectly as she seemed to try and decide what exactly it was he expected from her.

He searched her crystalline sapphire eyes before bending down and kissing her again. Her surprise was palpable; he could sense some fright underneath it as she remained unyielding against him for a moment more.

He believed the fear she felt was more from the unknowing of what he intended rather than the actual kiss. Then, to his surprise and delight, her lush mouth yielded, and he could feel the heat of her breath against his lips. He cradled her face as he pulled her closer to him, careful not to scare her as he deepened the kiss.

She was one of the most magnificent things he'd ever tasted. She was sweet and giving; her body warm against his as she yielded even more, pressing closer to him. He hadn't expected this from her. He had expected some resistance, a fight, but there was none of that.

In fact, she was far more receptive than he ever imagined she would be, and she felt far better than he thought possible. It felt right to hold her, to touch her. His hand entwined in her loose hair; it was as smooth as silk as it slid between his fingers.

Her hands curled around his forearms; a faint breath escaped her as he ran his tongue over her lips. To his surprise, her mouth parted further, granting him access to the sweet dark recesses.

He explored her mouth, pleasure overtaking him as her taste seemed to brand itself upon him. He couldn't stop the low groan of satisfaction escaping him as her tongue hesitantly, and then more boldly, met his.

He almost lifted her up and carried her from this room, but he knew he couldn't move too fast. She may be responding to him now, but she wouldn't continue to do so if he frightened her. And her ribs, he *had* to remember her ribs. He had to remind himself she was injured, but even as he thought it his control began to unravel, and his passion for her escalated sharply.

He pulled away before he couldn't. Pulled away before he lost complete control and either reinjured or scared her. He'd never felt this out of control, and though he'd never lost control of himself before, he realized it was a good possibility it could happen with her.

She unraveled him in strange ways, tested his restraint in ways it had never been tested before. She could make him a monster, or perhaps she could make him more human. He wasn't sure which thought unsettled him more.

The force of her breaths caused her chest to brush against his. Stroking her cheeks, he rested his forehead against hers. He savored the feel of her as he picked out the brighter flecks of blue within her turbulent eyes. He was trembling, nearly shaking with the effort it took for him not to kiss her again, not to taste the tempting blood coursing through her.

"I didn't expect that." Her voice shook as her grip on his arms intensified.

"Neither did I."

The admission rattled him as he brushed the hair gingerly back from her face. What was this girl to him? Why did she affect him so? What was going on here? The questions raced rapidly through his mind, but he couldn't answer any of them. There were no answers for him. He couldn't deny she was special, that he was supposed to have found her because he knew both of those things to be true.

He was, however, beginning to doubt he could keep her safe in his world, or even keep her safe from himself. This was not where she belonged. If anyone suspected he might have feelings for her, they would kill her. Blood slaves were used, drained, tortured, and tossed away. They were not treasured, they were not taken care of, and they most certainly were not kept alive for extended periods of time.

What was he going to do with her?

She peered questioningly up at him, her concern evident. He forced himself to become expressionless; she had obviously seen something that troubled her on his face.

"Prince?"

"Braith."

She blinked at him, her forehead furrowed in confusion. "Excuse me?" she asked in surprise.

"Braith, my name is Braith. You never say it. I want you to use it."

Her mouth quirked in a small smile, her eyes lit with amusement. "Forgive me, your majesty; I am not used to being around royalty."

Aggravation spurted through him at her words, until he realized she was teasing him. He had never been teased before, he wasn't sure he liked it, but it seemed to make her happy. He had to admit he enjoyed seeing her happy.

"I see. I would prefer if you said my name though," he told her abruptly.

His brisk attitude didn't seem to bother her as she shrugged her shoulders. The lack of fear she showed him was amazing; he had never experienced it before. Even other royal vampires were nervous and wary around him.

"Braith, why do you always wear those dark glasses?"

His hand darted up to the frames. For the most part, he didn't remember he was wearing them; they were like another extension of his body. He shrugged, unsure of how much he wanted to reveal to her. This situation was strange enough without heaping even more strange onto it.

Thankfully, he was saved from responding by a muted knock on the door. He released Arianna and took a step away before inviting whoever it was to enter. The small brunette he remembered seeing before stepped into the room. Braith bristled, his shoulders straightened as he prepared to take this girl on too.

Arianna rested her hand on his arm. He glanced at her, surprised by the calming effect such a simple gesture had on him.

"Hi, Maggie," she greeted, offering a small smile for the obviously frightened servant girl.

Maggie nodded at her, but her attention focused on Arianna's hand on his arm. Braith pulled away from Arianna, he wasn't trying to upset her, but they had to play it safe.

"I was told to come up," Maggie said hesitantly.

"Yes," Braith responded crisply. "Your friend was dismissed. Permanently." It took a moment for those words to sink in, but the implications of them affected her as he caught the increased beat of her heart. "The same will happen to you if you step out of line, in any way. You will take care with her ribs."

The girl looked stunned, and more than a little confused. "Yes, your Highness, of course, I will," she stammered out.

"Good."

Braith moved past the woman. Grabbing his cane, he left the room with Keegan trailing behind.

ARIA POPPED the grape into her mouth. She chewed the sweet fruit eagerly as she picked at the tray of food. She was starving from not eating yesterday. She heaped more fruit onto her plate, then some bread and meat. There was so much, and it all looked so good she didn't know where to start.

She tossed a handful of grapes into her mouth as she made her way to the window seat. She hadn't read in over a week, she'd missed it and was eager to continue with the story, but she planned to wait for Braith to come back. Aria worried she would get something confused when she read on her own, even though he said she was making good progress and was doing well on her own.

Truth be told, she merely enjoyed curling up next to him and listening to the deep rumble of his voice as he read with her. She stared out the window, rolling the fruit around in her mouth as she thought over the implications of that admission. Had becoming a blood slave caused her to lose her mind completely?

Was she beginning to have feelings for a monster? Did she have feelings for one of the creatures she had hated and fought against her entire life? That was crazy; it was simply insane. It couldn't be possible; it really couldn't.

But she truly believed she was, and she didn't understand any of it. She had thought he'd turned against her. That he had purposely set Lauren on her as punishment, but he hadn't. Not only had he not known Lauren was abusing her, but once he found out about it, he was attentive and caring, not to mention fiercely protective and worried about her safety.

And then he'd kissed her.

That kiss had almost been her undoing. She thought back to the kiss she'd shared with Max, it had been sweet and kind, and it had left her feeling safe and warm. Braith's kiss hadn't left her feeling any of those things. It had left her bewildered, on fire, and longing for *so* much more. She ached for him to hold her, and kiss her, and touch her forever. Yet it wasn't possible, none of it would *ever* be possible.

She chewed on a piece of cheese as she watched the sunlight play over the gardens. Though she didn't think he was, she knew there was still a possibility he was playing with her and toying with her emotions only to make her breakdown even more pleasurable in the end. But if that kiss was a sign of anything, she thought it was a sign he wouldn't purposely be cruel or mean to her.

She just didn't know exactly *what* he was going to be to her. She was far from certain of anything these days. A few weeks ago, she would have been terrified by this realization; she was surprised she wasn't scared now. She felt it was because of him. It was difficult to be frightened when he was watching over her.

Aria frowned as she realized she had never really been sheltered before. Her family loved her, and always tried to keep her safe, but she'd been on her own far more often than she was under their wing.

Children within the rebellion couldn't be coddled. Once they were old enough, they had to start helping out. Every hand was essential to feed the many hungry mouths and to help keep everyone safe.

Hunger, it was a foreign concept to her at the moment, as she munched on some more cheese and fruit. However, it wasn't a concept foreign to her family and friends right now. Guilt tugged at her; for a moment, she couldn't swallow the food as it stuck in her throat.

She was daydreaming about something that could never happen, a life she could never have with her enemy, and her family and friends were still struggling, still fighting for their lives every moment of every grueling day.

Aria managed to choke down the food, but she dropped her half-full plate back on the tray. Her appetite had vanished. Though she'd been given this reprieve from the famine, death, and struggle constituting most moments of her life, she knew it couldn't last.

His world would never allow it to last. She was a foolish child for thinking it might, a foolish child for not realizing the futility of this whole situation.

Aria touched the leather binding of the book; her fingers trailed leisurely over it as she admired the beauty of the thing. "Do you require me for anything else?"

Aria lifted her head; she'd forgotten Maggie was here. She'd been working on Aria's dresses; some of them had to be let out as she'd put on weight. "Oh no, thank you. Would you like something to eat?"

Maggie's mouth curved into a small smile as she shook her head. Though she hadn't commented upon the bruises marring Aria's skin, Aria had seen the distress and dismay in Maggie's tender gaze. Aria almost told her the injuries weren't from Braith, but the words stuck in her throat.

It was probably best if people began to believe he was mistreating her, though Lauren's dismissal might negate that fact. She imagined rumors and gossip were already flying about Lauren, and she found she didn't care.

"I have other things I must attend to."

"Oh." Aria felt a twinge of guilt over taking the girl away from her work. "I didn't mean to keep you."

"It's fine," Maggie assured her. "You are my number one priority. The prince has seen to that."

"I see."

"I'll see you later." Maggie was already at the door, her hand on the handle when she turned back to Aria. "The prince has never had a blood slave before, did you know that?"

Curiosity trickled through her as she stared at Maggie in disbelief. She recalled her encounter with Braith's sister. The woman had asked what he was doing with her. Aria thought the question odd at the time, had questioned if she *was* the first, but she'd never given much credit to the notion.

The revelation did little to ease the confusion inside her. In fact, it made it even worse. "I didn't know that."

Maggie nodded. "It's true."

Aria didn't know what to make of the words or their implication. Why would he choose one now? And why would he choose her?

Before Aria could ask any of these questions, Maggie slipped out the door, leaving her alone with her thoughts. She sighed as she settled on the window seat, torn and guilt-ridden. It was an awful mess she was in, that they *both* might be in. She didn't know all the rules for a blood slave, but she imagined she wasn't supposed to be treated so kindly. And she was fairly certain she wasn't supposed to stay alive for long.

That realization turned her thoughts back to Max. He was out there somewhere, probably going through something horrific and possibly on the verge of losing his life already. Sweet, gentle Max, he deserved far better than what he might be enduring right now. Max had vowed to try and rescue her, but they'd both known there was only a slim possibility for success.

Was there any chance she might be able to get to him?

Her gaze traveled over the beautiful apartment with all its magnificent things. She was lucky to be here, and that Braith rescued her from that other vile creature, but no matter how lucky she was, how good she had it, and how angry it would make Braith, she had to break free of this place.

She had to get to Max, and she had to get them both to safety before it was too late. Because no matter how safe and secure she felt now, it wouldn't last. It *couldn't* last.

It was only a matter of time before this all crumpled around her, and she had to do something before that happened. She had to save her friend before they were both doomed.

Her gaze slid back to the tray of food. If she was going to plan an escape, and free them both, then it was essential she had as much energy and strength as she could get. She couldn't afford to starve herself, but the idea of leaving Braith was enough to make her stomach twist

She needed the food, but there was no way she could force it down her throat right now. She was too frightened and lost to even attempt it. Tomorrow she would start taking better care of herself; for now, she sat in silent misery as she tried to formulate a plan to get out of here.

Though the stake was still tucked firmly between her breasts, she knew she wouldn't be able to bring herself to use it against the prince. She didn't have that in her, not anymore. No matter how much he exasperated and pissed her off, she knew she wouldn't be able to do that to him.

The first thing she had to do was locate Max. It would do her little good if she were able to break free, yet unable to find her friend. If she got out of here, she would have to know where he was so she could get to him safely. She knew it would be tricky, and she would have to move quickly, but she was fairly certain she would be able to do it.

She hoped.

Her attention was drawn to the door as Braith returned with his loyal wolf close to his side. She immediately knew something wasn't right. His shoulders were too stiff, and his jaw was clenched. Aria braced herself for whatever it was he had to say.

"Caleb will be here shortly. You must go to my room and stay there until I call for you."

Aria managed a brief nod. "Okay."

"Arianna." She turned back at the low murmur of her name. His knuckles were white as he gripped the head of his cane. "I mean it. Do not come out of there."

She almost rebelled against his command, but she kept her mouth shut. She didn't particularly care to see his brother again anyway; there was something about the man that frightened her on a primal level. She slipped silently from the room.

CHAPTER TEN

ARIA HATED the thin gold leash, but she accepted she had to wear it or she wouldn't be allowed to step foot outside. She wanted to be out of doors so badly she could almost taste it, wanted it so badly she was shaking with the need to breathe fresh air and feel it on her skin again.

It was also the only chance she had of maybe finding Max. Thankfully, she didn't have to argue with Braith as much as she'd thought to get him to take her into the town; she suspected he meant for people to see her chained to him as any other blood slave should be.

Aria ignored the questioning stares as Braith led her through the streets. Though she knew a rebel attack on the palace would be futile, she still tried to absorb as much detail as possible about the town within the palace confines. The cobblestone streets were clean and lined with beautiful buildings, which it took her awhile to realize, were homes.

Vampires moved about the streets; many had blood slaves meekly following behind. The gold leash was the brightest thing about the unfortunate victims trudging behind their masters.

Aria tried not to stare at the blood slaves, tried not to notice the melancholy they radiated, but by the time they made it a few hundred feet down the road she had tears in her eyes.

These slaves were thin, beaten, marred with bruises and bite marks. Some looked healthier than others, but the bleak look in all their eyes shook her. These were her people, and they were being cruelly used and slowly bled to death.

Braith had saved her from such a fate, but she had come very close to sharing their same end. That thought didn't ease the anguish clawing at her, but only increased it. She was no better than any of these people; she didn't deserve to be spared when they hadn't been.

Braith grabbed her elbow, pulling her close against him. "Do not cry; do not show sympathy, if you do, then we must go back. You are not permitted to show such emotions; do you understand me?" he hissed in her ear.

Aria bowed her head as she tried to blink away the hot sting of tears burning her eyes. How could she not show sympathy for these poor, broken people that were suffering unfairly? Braith released her arm; he took an abrupt step away from her as they neared the busier market section of the town.

Vampires and free people mingled about the shops and stores, merchants selling their wares in the streets shouted to be heard above the bustle of activity. Aria's eyes darted over everything; there was no way she could take it all in.

She had never seen anything like it in her life, never even imagined such a place existed. They had so much here, while so many others had so little. The greed and selfishness overwhelmed her. Rage trickled through her, her feelings of helplessness swelled to the point of nearly choking her.

"Amazing," she muttered, trying not to reveal the antipathy rising within her.

She felt Braith's eyes on her, but she didn't look at him again.

She abruptly stopped as they rounded the top of a hill. Her breath froze in her lungs, a feeling of homesickness tore through her with such intensity that her legs nearly gave out. Over the top of the walls, beyond the town nestled in the valley below the palace, were the woods.

Her woods.

Shaking, her fingers curled as she took a step forward. For a moment, she could almost feel the cool shade of the leafy trees, touch their roughened bark, and smell the earthy scent of leaves and dirt. For a moment, she was there, with her family. For a second she was happy, for just one small moment, she was *home*.

Then reality slapped her harshly in the face, and she was back in the crowded market area of the palace town, leashed to a vampire that owned her, and surrounded by her enemy.

She wasn't free; she hadn't been free in a while and may never be free again. She was far from the forest and the people she had grown up with. She felt broken and hollow; even the stable presence of Braith by her side did little to ease the home-sickness festering within her chest.

The crowd parted as he led her through it. Everyone scurried to get out of his, and Keegan's, way. Aria trailed silently behind, acting like the docile and good blood slave she was supposed to be, though now she didn't have to work too hard to act the part.

She was too upset to keep up with his brisk, purposeful strides. Her eyes darted over everyone, rapidly searching for Max or the woman who claimed him somewhere amongst the crush of bodies.

Aria stopped short as they broke free of the crowd, immediately revolted and somewhat nauseated as she came face to face with the stage she was paraded around. She felt the sharp tug of her leash, but her feet wouldn't move as she gazed at the newest victims huddled on the simple platform. The same man who auctioned her off was spewing the praises of the young boy he held.

"Move!" a sharp shove pushed her forward, knocking her momentarily off balance. She barely caught a glance of the woman who shoved her out of the way.

Aria managed to get her feet to move again. She stumbled forward, suddenly finding it difficult to breathe in the packed street. Braith had been stopped by an older man with graying hair and a potbelly. The fact he was a human traitor only irritated her more. The man's hands fluttered all around as he spoke rapidly.

The man didn't acknowledge her presence, but she did see his gaze flicker to the golden leash. Aria turned away, trying to ignore the chain keeping her tied to Braith. She fought hard to keep her emotions in check, but she resented that Keegan roamed free while she was tethered.

This was the way it was supposed to be; this was the only way a blood slave could be brought out in public. He couldn't allow her to roam free; too many questions would be raised then.

Even as she reminded herself of this, she bristled against the fact this was her life for however much time it would be granted to her. She had accepted death when she first arrived here; she'd hoped and prayed for it. She didn't want to accept it now though.

A tug on her leash alerted her to the fact Braith was ready to move on. She turned back to him, freezing instantly as her eyes latched onto the woman who had claimed Max. She was a few feet away from Braith and honing in on him.

She was just as beautiful as Aria remembered with her flowing hair and voluptuous figure. Aria had the fleeting thought this was the type of woman, or vampire, Braith desired. She didn't know why the idea popped into her head, but once it was there, it festered like a thorn.

"Prince," the woman greeted, a knowing smile curving her full mouth as she thrust her hip out and batted her lashes.

Aria had to fight the urge to glare at the blatant, obnoxious woman. Annoyance and jealousy curdled through her as the woman touched Braith's arm. There was a familiarity between them that shook her. She didn't like other women around him, but worse, she *really* didn't like that such a realization troubled her so much.

Though Braith didn't move closer to the woman, the overt way she pressed herself against him nearly caused Aria to vomit. That was all she could take. Turning sharply away, her gaze scanned the crowd as she eagerly sought out Max. She spotted him almost instantly, standing amongst the crush of bodies, his golden leash draped over a wooden post with other blood slaves tied to it as if they were horses.

Aria's stomach dropped, her heart leapt in her chest as she gazed at her friend. A surge of relief and hope erupted in her chest. The sight of him was one of the most amazing things she'd ever encountered. The moment her eyes found him, he also saw her.

Relief filled his bright blue eyes as he stepped toward her, only to be brought up short by the leash holding him in place. Tears filled her eyes; he still looked healthy, but the broken air surrounding him robbed her of her breath. Bite marks marred his neck and arms, and there was a fading bruise on his cheek.

Without thinking, she moved toward him, needing to touch and speak with a man who meant so much to her. Max grabbed the leash, looking as if he would rip it free, but they both knew that was impossible.

His mouth parted as delight radiated from him. Aria couldn't help but smile back; her fingers itched to touch him as her heart soared with happiness. For one brief, shining moment, everything was right, and she didn't know despair. She only knew she had to get to her friend.

Aria was pulled back a few inches when her leash was tugged

sharply. She turned, about to vent her frustration when she realized Braith stood right behind her. That muscle was throbbing in his cheek again; his shoulders squared as he loomed over her. When he turned his attention to Max, his nostrils flared.

Aria could feel the anger coursing through him, but she didn't understand the intensity of it. He wrapped his hand sternly around her leash, drawing her closer as he pulled the golden cord taut between them.

Aria couldn't stop her gaze from going back to Max. She just wanted to speak with him, to know if he was okay, to have one moment where she could talk with her friend and reconnect with something familiar, something she missed so badly.

She realized she'd made a mistake. Braith's knuckles were white as he wrapped the chain around his wrist. A slip of paper couldn't separate them anymore. Though no one around them seemed to have noticed her encounter with Max, even the woman who owned Max had been distracted by some jewelry, it was obvious Braith hadn't missed it.

"Braith—"

"Your Highness," he corrected sharply.

Aria shrank back as hurt bloomed in her chest. She wanted to tell him something that would make the look of betrayal leave his face. That would make the wrath simmering just below the surface abate a little.

She didn't think he was in the mood to listen to her, and she didn't know how to start explaining anything amongst this crowd. She wasn't sure what she *had* to explain to him, or why he was so irate with her. She hadn't done anything wrong.

Aria stared helplessly up at him. The woman appeared at his side again, drawing his attention away from Aria. They spoke briefly, but Aria didn't hear a word they said. Despite her best efforts not to, her gaze slid back to Max. Her heart sank; tears of hopelessness swam in her eyes.

In his gaze, she could see the terrible despair of their situation; the complete realization they were trapped. And yet, she could also see a burgeoning fury within him as his attention turned back to Braith. True hatred simmered within Max's eyes.

For the first time, she was completely frightened of this whole mess. She had tried to convince herself it would all work out in the end; that somehow they would escape. She realized now they never would. They would die here, and there was nothing either of them could do to stop it.

A hand wrapped around her arm; she knew instantly it was Braith's as her skin came alive, and her entire body reacted to his touch. She couldn't bring herself to look at him as the hated woman slipped past her. Aria wouldn't have been surprised to learn she and Braith had made plans to meet up later. She knew what Braith was, what he required, and he wasn't asking her for any of it.

She hated her sense of betrayal, hated everything about this awful place and this horrendous day. She'd never coveted the simplicity of her woods and caves more than she did right now.

She lifted her gaze to Braith, but he was no longer looking at her. In fact, he looked like he wanted to completely forget her existence as he released her arm and glided through the parting crowd. Aria hurried to keep up with him as he strode purposely forward, nearly dragging her behind him.

She looked back at Max, struggling against the tears burning her eyes. She was terrified this may be the last chance she would ever have to see him. He watched her closely; his face dark with fury.

*

ARIA WAS NEARLY breathless by the time Braith hauled her into his apartment. He radiated rage but somehow managed to shut the door silently.

"Braith—"

"Your Highness," he grated.

Aria recoiled as if slapped. She could understand why she was supposed to call him that in public, but they were alone now and there was no one near to question them.

"What?" she managed to sputter out.

"I told you to call me Your Highness."

Aria gaped after him as he released her leash and strode across the room. She was well aware he hadn't removed the loathsome golden chain from her wrist. She stared dejectedly at the thin strand, wondering if it would ever come off again. She was afraid it might not, and as long as it was on her, she would never be able to break free of this awful place.

He'd told her the chain was linked to him, that he could find it anywhere, and he was the only one who could ever remove it from her. She would like to believe that wasn't true, but she suspected it was.

She'd been completely wrong about him; he was just as cold and cruel as everyone else in this hideous place. She folded her free hand over the top of the golden chain, itching to rip the offending thing from her skin.

She'd heard rumors, stories that if a slave tried to pull the chain free, it would slice through their skin, tearing into the flesh. Their blood would run freely, staining the gold. It was the reason the leash was also known as the blood chain.

At the moment, Aria didn't care.

Terror drove her as she dug at it, trying to rip it free. She didn't care her flesh shredded, didn't feel the pain, or notice the blood spilling freely down her fingers and wrist. She only wanted out of this thing and to have her life back. She didn't want to be someone's captive anymore, someone's *thing* to use and order about as they saw fit.

Braith's hands seized her. A strangled cry escaped her lips as she tried to rip her hands free of his grasp, but he clung to her. She jerked wildly, resentment and frustration boiling in her veins. She was tired of living in this place and playing by *his* rules, tired of being ordered about and having her entire life dictated over.

"Let go of me!" she cried.

"Stop it!" he snarled, pulling her toward him. "You're injuring yourself, Arianna."

"You're hurting me!" she snapped back, fighting to escape his hold. "I'd rather be dead then trapped like this! Why didn't you let me die? Why don't you just kill me and get it over with?"

He pulled her hand away from the leash, thrusting it down to his side and pinning it there. "Enough!" he barked. "You would prefer to die than be separated from your lover?"

Outrage froze her as she gaped at him. "How dare you!" she spat.

He released her hand, tossing it away in abhorrence as he stepped back.

"You know nothing of me!" she yelled. "Nothing of my life! Nothing of who I am! You sit in this palace, where you've had everything handed to you, and judge those who refuse to be beaten down and broken by your rules, your poor treatment, and your death sentences! You have no right to judge me!"

His dark eyebrows lifted sharply; his jaw clenched and unclenched as a vein throbbed in his forehead. She could feel his revulsion as his lip curled into a sneer. "There isn't much of you to judge."

Acting on pure instinct, and with the reckless abandonment her father often cautioned her about, Aria's hand snaked up his side with the agility and speed that had kept her alive for the past seventeen years. That same recklessness would probably be what brought about the end of her life now as her hand connected with his face.

The slap echoed in the deathly silence following. Aria panted as she glared furiously at him. The mark of her bloody handprint was evident against the hard curve of his cheek.

His head, which was knocked slightly aside by her violent blow, slowly came back to her. His mouth parted as he stared at her for a long moment. Beneath his astonishment though, she could sense the growing wrath building within him.

She should be scared; she wasn't. She should probably beg for his forgiveness; she wouldn't.

She didn't give a damn what he said or did to her anymore. She almost welcomed this as she sensed it was the end. One way or another, there would finally be an end to all this unknowing.

He stepped into her, forcing her against the wall, his face mere inches from hers. Aria's hands shook as she awaited her inevitable fate. His hands rested on either side of her head as he bent low, his nose nearly touching hers.

He vibrated with rage as his lips peeled back to reveal the sharp edge of his now elongated canines. Her pulse escalated as she focused on those fangs. It was the first time she'd seen them fully extended, and she was certain they were about to destroy her.

"It won't be *you* I kill, Arianna," he snarled.

Her knees buckled as the implication of his words sank in.

"I'll keep you alive, and I'll make you watch as I relish *his* slow death," Braith vowed. "I can take whatever I want, *whenever* I want it. I have been kind to you so far; I won't be kind anymore. *No* one disobeys me; *no* one goes against me. I will show you what kind of a monster I can truly be."

"No," she managed to whisper.

"Oh yes, and I am going to enjoy it. I'm actually rather parched; it's been awhile since I've fed."

Horror tore through her; she rapidly shook her head as he shoved away from her and swept toward the door. She knew where he was going and who he was after. She had to stop him. Max would be punished because she was an idiot. She couldn't allow that to happen. Not again.

"Wait! No! Stop! Your Highness, please don't do this! Please!" She scurried after him, nearly tripping over the leash still tethered to her. She seized his hand, but he shook her off like a bug. "Don't do this! Braith, I'm begging you!"

Her feet tangled up in the leash, jerking her awkwardly down, and causing it to slice deeper into her flesh.

"He's my friend! He's been my friend since we were children! He's like a brother to me!" Despair threatened to choke her as tears clogged her throat. "I have *never* begged for anything from anyone in my life, but I am begging you; please don't kill him! He did nothing wrong! I'm sorry. I'll do whatever you ask, whenever you ask it of me! Punish me! Punish *me*!"

The force of her sobs made it almost impossible for her to breathe through her broken rib. She couldn't move; agony racked her entire body. The blood spilling from her wounds formed a puddle beneath her and soaked into her dress, but she didn't care. She didn't care about anything anymore.

She'd destroyed Max's life. She hadn't freed him; instead, she'd given him a death sentence, and from the look on Braith's face, it would be a long and tortured process.

There was a long moment of silence in which she couldn't look at him. She felt as if her misery would kill her. Then, to her surprise, she felt the gentlest touch she'd ever experienced. His hands cradled her cheeks as he lifted her face to his.

His lips brushed her cheeks, her forehead, whispering against her ear as he tried to soothe her. Aria's mind spun as his hands and mouth caressed her with a tenderness that nearly undid the horror of the past half an hour.

"Don't," he said.

The word slid over her skin making her body tingle with electricity at the same time it completely undid her. Her sobs rocked her as a low moan escaped her. She didn't know why she was crying now, didn't know where the source of this distress came from, but Aria could no more stem the flow of them than she could tether the wind.

"Arianna, stop, you'll injure yourself more. Stop, Arianna, it's okay."

His hands were in her hair, drawing her against him as he wrapped his arms around her and rocked her against his chest.

CHAPTER ELEVEN

ARIA REMAINED mute as Braith bandaged her wrist. His hands were feather light on her mutilated and sore skin. Her tears had finally subsided, but she felt exhausted and defeated. He was being kind to her again, and she didn't know why.

Neither of them had spoken in the past hour. Why had he come back to her? What stopped him from going after Max?

Ultimately, as long as Max was spared, she didn't care what the reasons were. She'd promised Braith anything he asked of her, and she meant it.

Was that promise what brought him back? She wasn't going to risk him changing his mind. She'd overestimated his kindness and understanding of her, hadn't thought there was a snapping point within him, but then again, she hadn't slapped him before either. She supposed she was lucky he hadn't killed her outright.

When he finished with her bandages, his hand rested on her wrapped wrist and fingers.

She lifted her head to meet his shaded eyes. "Why?" she inquired.

"Why what?"

She gulped, wary of sending him into another frenzy, but she knew she had to ask the question. "Why did you pull me off that stage? Why did you choose me when you've never had a blood slave before?"

His hands gently squeezed hers before he rose from the floor and sat on the bed beside her. "I see people have been talking."

She fiddled anxiously with her bandages. "I think most are curious."

"As are you?"

"As am I," she agreed.

He was silent for a moment as his attention fixed on the doorway. "I have never had a blood slave before because I prefer to take my blood from the willing. Many of my kind enjoy the force and the control; I do not. I never have."

Her fingers stilled on her bandages as she studied his handsome countenance. He had wiped her blood from his face, but she could still see her rapidly fading, reddened handprint. A small bit of shame crept through her; she shouldn't have hit him, but she'd never been one to control her temper. It nearly cost Max his life.

"There are many willing ones out there?" she asked.

She felt his eyes slide over her. She could only imagine what she must look like. Her eyes had to be bloodshot; she could feel the swelling in them. She assumed her face was blotchy and puffy also. Her hair was wild as it straggled around her face.

Her appearance never mattered to her before though, and it didn't matter now. There was a reason she was here, even if he was hesitant to reveal it, and she knew it had nothing to do with her looks.

"Yes," he said.

She didn't like the strange pit forming in her stomach as he confirmed what she already knew.

What was wrong with her? Just an hour ago she'd slapped

him; now she was upset by the thought of him with other women. She had finally flipped her lid, and she was surprised to realize she didn't care. Not anymore.

"So then why me? Why did you choose *me?*" she asked.

He ran a hand through his hair. It was already disheveled, and now it stood on end a little. He stood up and walked over to the window before moving back across the room. He looked like a caged animal as he paced restlessly back and forth.

Tension and power thrummed through him, and for the first time she saw him for what he was. He wasn't a man, or a vampire, and certainly not her enemy. He was someone who was as confused and uncertain about this situation as she was.

"Because I *saw* you on that stage," he said.

Aria frowned; unsure how to respond to it. What did *that* mean? Of course, he'd seen her on the stage, as had everyone else present that day. "I don't understand."

"No, of course, you don't," he muttered. Stopping before her, he knelt to take her hands. "I brought you here because, for the first time in almost a hundred years, I was able to see something, and that something was *you, Arianna.*"

Her fingers were limp in his as she stared at him in confusion. Her eyes scanned his face before landing on the thick glasses. Her mind flashed to the cane, and Keegan, ever present at Braith's side.

"You're blind," she breathed, awed by this revelation, and the fact she hadn't realized it earlier. But he couldn't be blind. How could he have taught her to read? And how had she always felt his gaze on her? How had he seen her connection with Max today if he was blind? "I don't understand."

He shook his head before turning to look out the window. "I don't either," he admitted. "But for some reason, I saw you on that stage, and once the amazement of actually *seeing* something again wore off, I realized I could also see the things around you."

"So your vision is coming back?"

"No." He turned back to her. "I only see things when you are near. When I leave this room, when I'm not in your presence, I'm still unable to see."

Aria's heart leapt wildly in her chest. She didn't know what to make of this confession or what it signified. Her heart raced as she leaned forward and touched the edge of his glasses. He didn't move away from her, didn't stop her as her fingers wrapped around them. She bit her lip; excitement washed over her as she pulled the glasses away.

His eyes were closed, but she could see faint white scars outlining them. It had been a hundred years, plenty of time for a vampire to heal, but those scars still marred his otherwise perfect, masculine beauty. Her fingers stroked over the marks as compassion washed over her. Whatever caused this had to be something horrific to leave this type of lasting damage.

"Let me see, Braith." Her words were barely a whisper as she was consumed by the sudden need to see his eyes.

His eyes remained closed for a moment before his long, dark lashes swept upward. Surprise flickered through her as she found herself frozen in the grip of his turbulent stare.

His eyes were striking. The striking gray of them robbed her of her breath. Around the iris was an arresting band of bright blue color. Though his eyes focused on her, they seemed strangely unseeing and somewhat dazed as she ran her fingers over the scars encircling them.

Even though they were damaged, his were the most beautiful eyes she'd ever seen.

"Beautiful." She saw the brief shock that rolled through him, but she didn't care. They were beautiful, and she couldn't stop touching him. "What happened?"

"An explosion."

"The war?" He shook his head in response but didn't elaborate, and she sensed he didn't plan to. She wasn't going to push him either. It didn't matter how it occurred; it simply mattered she was here, with him. "I'm sorry."

"It was years ago; I'd long since adapted to the loss. Until you."

She stopped searching his damaged gaze and focused on the man before her. "What does it all mean?"

His hands encircled hers; his grasp was tender on her wounded fingers. "I don't know what it means, Arianna. I wish I had more answers, but I don't. I do know I wasn't going to let you go once I saw you, and I especially wasn't going to let you go to Richard Ellis."

She pressed her hands tighter against his face as she leaned forward and brushed her lips tenderly against his forehead. She wished she could heal the damage inflicted on him. Aria couldn't undo what was done to him all those years ago, long before she was even born, but she could attempt to soothe the lingering anguish she sensed in him now.

"Braith," she breathed, so completely lost and confused by everything happening to her. To them.

She pulled back, surprised to feel tears burning her eyes again. She didn't think she could possibly have any more tears left in her, but she did.

"Arianna, you must listen to me. I don't mean to hurt you, I really don't, but there are rules to being a blood slave, and there are rules about the relationship of a master and their slave."

"I know my life isn't going to be a lengthy one," she assured him. "I've known that for years. I've seen more death than people three times my age, and I've narrowly avoided it many, *many* times. I understand the rules, Braith; and I know there's nothing you can do—"

"But there is, or there could be, but you must do as I say, Arianna. Other vampires have kept slaves for a few years. But you must behave, you *must* stay quiet, and you have to stay away from your lover—"

"Max is just my friend!" she interrupted sharply, angry he kept insisting on something that wasn't true. "I told you that already, and I meant it. We've been together since we were children; he's my brother's best friend. If it wasn't for me and my recklessness, Max wouldn't be here. I can't let him suffer because I'm a fool who never listens to orders..."

Aria broke off; she silently cursed herself as she realized what she'd nearly revealed to him. Something was growing and changing between them, but there were some things she could never admit. Even if he didn't plan to harm her, there were others who would still use her against her family, and that was something she could never let happen.

"Orders?" he asked.

She shook her head, unwilling to discuss this now. She simply couldn't. "Max is my friend, and he is going to die because of me. I can't... I can't bear it," she choked out. "All he wanted was to save me, for Daniel."

"Daniel?"

Aria managed a tremulous smile. "My brother."

Braith's face was rigid, his eyes searching as he looked her over. "I see."

"Max could have gotten away, Braith. I went in to rescue Mary's child, but Max could have gotten away. He could have fled into the woods. He's here because he thought he could save me from all of this; Max is an optimist to the end."

"And you're not?"

She managed a feeble smile. "I've always been one hundred percent pragmatic. As I said, I've seen a lot in my short life, very little of it has been good. Max *is* good though, and I hate that his goodness will be destroyed because of me. I didn't mean to hurt you; I just wanted to see my friend, to know he was safe, and that he wasn't dead... at least not yet anyway."

Braith stretched his long legs before him as he sat back. "You didn't hurt me."

When Aria's hands slipped away from his face, they brushed against the stubble already lining his jaw. "Of course, I didn't hurt you. I shouldn't have said that; I didn't mean it."

She couldn't hurt him; she'd been foolish to think maybe that was the reason he'd been so angry with her over Max. She had to remember that, although her feelings for him might be changing, his feelings for her were still inscrutable.

"I didn't mean to do what I did today. When I saw Max, he reminded me so much of home, and I missed him so much that all I could think about was getting to him. All I could think of was my woods and hunting and running free. *Freedom*, Braith, I loved my freedom. I'm sorry that what I did today could have caused us both problems, but I couldn't stop myself because for one moment, I was in the woods again. I could smell the forest, taste it, feel it around me, and it was wonderful."

Aria broke off, overcome with a crushing sense of homesickness again. Braith was silent as he studied her, and then his fingers were in her hair, and he was pulling her against him. Aria gasped as his mouth claimed hers with a desperation that left her dazed and breathless. At first, she was so surprised she remained motionless against him, unable to respond to the intensity and passion she felt radiating from him.

Then the torrent of emotions surging forth in her buried her shock. She was rocked by the need filling her and the desperation that seized her. She needed *him*.

It all felt so astonishingly right! Something inside her was healing and becoming whole. There had always been something missing in her life, something she'd been searching and hoping for, but she'd never known what it was. Until now.

Now, with his mouth on hers, her body tingling with electricity and a fire building within her, she knew it was *him*.

He was what she'd been missing; *he* was what she'd been searching for. His absence was what made her so reckless all the time. Because without him, she'd been so lost and empty she hadn't stopped to think about the consequences of her actions. She knew there would be consequences for these actions, but she didn't care.

She'd always hated and fought against his kind, but she thought this might be the first right thing she'd *ever* done.

His large body loomed over hers as he seized her waist and lifted her easily up to deposit her in the center of the bed. Her heart hammered; excitement and nervousness tore through her in equal measures as he came down on top of her.

She couldn't get enough of the feel of him. His chest was firm against hers, the width of his shoulders nearly three times the size of hers as his arm wrapped around her waist and he lifted her against him.

The differences in their bodies were startling, he was unbending everywhere she was yielding, and yet she fit perfectly against him. Her curves hugged all the right places of his rock-solid frame.

When she gasped, he took advantage of the small exhalation escaping her to take full possession of her mouth. He tasted of spices as his tongue slid into her mouth in a sensual dance that left her aching for more. When his shirt bunched up, her fingers fell against the bare skin at the hollow of his lower back.

Her hands splayed over the rigid muscles flexing beneath her palms as he settled more firmly between her legs. He kissed her breathless, kissed her until she couldn't think straight and was desperate for more.

His strong hands slipped the thin dress up her thighs. His fingers brushed against her bare skin, stroking her as he moved steadily higher. She wanted to scream with pleasure at the same time a bolt of fear shot through her. It was all so new and thrilling, but it was also moving far too fast as the heavy weight of his body pressed her deeper into the mattress.

Aria broke free of the enchanting pressure of his mouth when reality crashed around her. She couldn't breathe, couldn't control her surging body and tumultuous emotions.

"Wait, Braith, wait," she managed to pant out.

He froze against her; his fingers a tantalizing sensation as they stilled on her thigh. It was the most intimate touch she'd ever experienced. A tremor raced through her as desire sent her heartbeat skyrocketing again. She'd never felt such overwhelming desire and belonging mingled with such pulsating dread of the unknown. She couldn't think, and she desperately needed a minute to at least try and sort out what was going on.

His hands were on her face, turning it towards him. She blinked at him as she focused on the beautiful, caring eyes before her. "Arianna, are you okay?"

She managed a wan smile. "I'm just... I'm not... It's too fast. It's all too fast."

His eyes scanned questioningly over her face. Then, much to her dismay, a dawning realization seemed to come over him. His brow smoothed out; his eyes were far more understanding as they came back to her.

"Arianna, are you a virgin?"

Her face flooded with color, and her eyes darted rapidly away from him. She was too mortified to meet his gaze again.

"Why didn't you tell me?" he asked.

She bit her bottom lip as she struggled to keep the fierce heat from her face.

"You should have told me," he said. "I would have gone slower; I would have—"

"Stop," she whispered, too embarrassed to hear any more.

He bent his head to press his forehead against hers. His lips were swollen from their kisses as they hovered over hers; seeming to breathe her in even though he didn't require air. His fingers played with her hair.

"Okay," he said, pressing a quick peck to her nose.

Rolling off her, he pulled her against his side. Aria was enthralled by the easiness with which he embraced her, and the fact he'd taken her abrupt stop so calmly. His fingers were as soft as down against her wounded ribs; the light pressure felt good.

"I don't understand any of this," she whispered.

He brushed the hair back from her face and tilted her chin up to him. "Neither do I, but you must keep this to yourself, Arianna. No one else can know about my eyesight."

"Not even your family?"

"They see my blindness as a weakness, and many would like to keep me weak. If they realize I have my vision back, and that it's because of *you*, they'll kill you to keep me weak. They may not know why I can only see around you, and they won't care. You can't let anyone know."

"I won't," she promised.

He smiled at her as he pressed tender kisses across her cheeks. She was amazed by him, overjoyed by the tenderness he showed her, staggered he so readily accepted being denied something he craved. He was a vampire, and yet she knew now that though he could be volatile, he wasn't a monster. He never would be, not to her anyway. She knew it with every fiber of her being.

"What are you going to do with me?" she asked.

His eyes twinkled brightly as a small dimple briefly flashed in his right cheek. "Whatever you would like me to do."

Aria couldn't help but smile back at him as she traced the ridge of his jaw.

"I know you covet your freedom, Arianna, and I understand that, but I can't give it to you. I will keep you protected for as long as I can, but although I am a prince, there are still those with more power than me. It may take a little while, but I will work through this, somehow. I won't let them kill you."

Aria nodded, warmed by his words, but not at all comforted by them. There would be little either of them could do if it were decided she was a threat that must be eliminated.

"You look exhausted," he said.

"I am," she admitted.

"Sleep, we can talk later."

She didn't want to sleep; she enjoyed lying there and feeling him against her. She wanted to experience the awe of her strange and tenuous situation. Although she fought against it, sleep was swift and deep when it finally claimed her.

CHAPTER TWELVE

BRAITH WATCHED the light play off Arianna's vibrant hair. Her head was bent; her legs drawn up beneath her as she sat curled within the window seat. She had moved on from *Ivanhoe* and now held, *Of Mice and Men*, before her.

Her instincts were well honed; she had managed to slap him after all, but she hadn't noticed his arrival. He was able to observe her enthrallment of the novel.

She may not be the most elegant or refined woman, but the longer he stared at her, the more he realized that to him, she was the most beautiful woman he'd ever seen and always would be. Braith felt a strange surge of emotion as he watched her; it was an emotion he'd never experienced before, and one he couldn't figure out right now.

She finally realized he was there as she lifted her head and blinked at him in surprise. The small smile spreading across her face lit her delicate features and sparkled in her sapphire eyes.

She swung her feet down and placed the book beside her as she rose. Her wrist and fingers were still bandaged; the white cotton a stark contrast against the golden hue of her skin.

She was mouthwatering, alluring without meaning to be, beautiful without even trying, and she was *his*. The possessive feeling was so overwhelming it almost consumed him. At that moment, he knew it was true, he knew she was his, and he would do everything in his power to keep her safe.

"Hello," she said.

Her gaze darted shyly away as her cheeks flooded with color. He'd left her sleeping this morning, unwilling to wake her after the events of yesterday. Now her uncertainty raced to the forefront as she fiddled with the bandages and shifted nervously.

"Arianna," he greeted, smiling as he placed his cane next to the door. It was astonishing to see once again, but the best thing was seeing *her*. Keegan padded into the room and settled by her feet. Braith hadn't missed the fact that even the wolf seemed infatuated with her. "Did you eat?"

She nodded; her smile was tremulous as she looked at the tray of food. He could almost see the wheels spinning within her mind, as more than thoughts of food crossed it. Her expression cleared as she met his gaze again.

He could sense the questions lingering beneath her calm exterior, but she didn't ask him about where he was eating as he suspected she wanted to ask him. It surprised him when she held her tongue; it was a first since he'd met her.

"Arianna?"

She smiled at him, but the smile didn't reach her eyes. "This book is really good."

He glanced at the novel resting on the seat before pulling his coat off and rolling his tense shoulders. He tossed his coat over the rack by the door. He could guess at what troubled her, but if she didn't choose to speak about it, then he wasn't going to force her to.

Where he was getting his blood supply from wasn't something he cared to discuss anyway. He wasn't going to make her do anything she wasn't willing to do, but he still had to feed, even if he found the women he took blood from undesirable now, and it was really *her* blood he craved. He had to sate his thirst elsewhere. Otherwise, he might injure her without meaning to.

"It is one of my favorites stories," he said.

She watched him as he walked toward her. He was itching to touch her again, to feel her once more. Her head tilted back as she stared at him and her breath came more rapidly. He could hear the increased beat of her heart; smell her increased passion. He smiled at her, pleased to know he affected her as much as she affected him.

He caressed her face, his hand twining into her thick hair. She was the most breathtaking thing he'd ever seen. Bending over her, he pressed a soft kiss to her full lips. His arm encircled her waist, and he lifted her against him, holding her tight as she wrapped her arms around his neck.

It amazed him how incredible she felt and how right all of this was. Like the missing piece of a puzzle, she blended seamlessly against him, melding to him in all the right places.

How on earth had it come to this? That *he*, of all vampires, had managed to find himself in this situation, ensnared by the allure of a human. A *rebel* human. It was unthinkable, and at the moment he didn't care as he lost himself to the feel of her mouth and body against his.

He was so lost to her that he didn't hear the knock on the door until it was too late. Keegan's low growl alerted him to someone's presence. Braith froze; his hands stilled on Arianna as he pulled slightly away from her.

Dazed passion still darkened her eyes as a blush colored her face. Though Braith couldn't see his brother, he knew it was Caleb who entered. He could feel the force of Caleb's gaze boring into his back.

"Don't let me interrupt you, brother," Caleb purred as he closed the door behind him. "You know I don't mind."

Apprehension shot through Arianna's eyes. Her appalled gaze darted toward Caleb, but Braith held her still as he kept her sheltered from Caleb's scrutiny. A scrutiny he knew would be cruel, and far more leering than Braith wanted her exposed to.

He held her for a moment more before sliding her gradually back to the ground. How had he missed Caleb's approach?

He usually sensed his brother the moment he hit the hallway. The wave of cruelty Caleb emanated was impossible to miss.

"Go to my room," Braith instructed Arianna.

"By all means, continue," Caleb drawled. "I'll wait. I'd even enjoy watching."

Horror bloomed in Arianna's gaze; she tried again to look at Caleb, but Braith held the back of her head.

"Arianna," he growled.

Her attention came back to him; her lips, still swollen from his kiss, trembled. He could sense her revulsion. He wished he could shelter her from his brother, but it was too late for that. Caleb was amongst them now, and he was one of the nastiest sons of a bitches Braith had ever known. He didn't like Caleb anywhere near Arianna.

"Go," Braith commanded.

She hesitated before nodding. He released her and stepped back. Arianna squared her shoulders and locked her jaw. She kept her chin raised as she strode across the room, not looking at Caleb as she moved.

"Wait!" Caleb commanded.

Braith didn't want anyone ordering her around, least of all his little brother, but he couldn't do much without possibly exposing his growing feelings for her. Arianna stopped; her head turned toward Caleb, and she kept her shoulders back. Amusement flitted over Caleb's face, but Braith saw the depravity in his brother's gaze as it raked over Arianna.

"She's not really your type, Braith, not that you can see that, but she's not. I, on the other hand, have always liked a redhead. I think you should give me a turn at her."

Disgust flashed across Arianna's face; her gaze darted frantically toward Braith. He hated she was being exposed to this, hated his brother for doing it to her, but he couldn't stop it. If he did, her life would surely be forfeit.

"I don't share," Braith stated.

Caleb folded his arms over his chest as his gaze leisurely raked Arianna from head to toe again. "Anymore," Caleb purred. "Things were different just a month ago."

"Go!" Braith snarled at her as he fought the urge to punch his brother in the face.

Amusement flickered over Caleb's handsome features, but he didn't try to stop Arianna again as she hurried from the room. Though she hid it well, Braith could sense her confusion and fear over Caleb's statements.

Braith kept his attention on his brother. He grappled to keep his temper under control and his face impassive. He wasn't sure he succeeded though as Caleb stared questioningly at him. A gaze he didn't realize Braith could now see.

"What are you doing here, Caleb?" he inquired when he heard the faint click of the door closing behind Arianna.

His vision darkened without her beside him, but still dimly made out his brother. Caleb shrugged as he moved into the room and settled himself leisurely on one of the sofas. Braith bristled but didn't show any reaction to his brother's cavalier attitude.

"Father has decided to hold a banquet tonight," Caleb said

"Why?"

Caleb draped his arm over the back of the couch as he stretched his long legs before him. "Jericho has returned."

Braith stiffened; Keegan padded over to brush against his legs as he sensed Braith's sudden turmoil.

"And do you know what it means if little brother has returned?" Caleb inquired.

"The war will resume," Braith answered as his gaze darted toward the closed door. He didn't want Arianna to know about this, not yet anyway.

"Yes," Caleb agreed. "I wonder what he has learned."

Braith didn't respond; there was no use in trying to guess what Jericho learned during his time away. He hadn't agreed with Jericho being sent out to attempt assimilating with the rebels in the first place.

Jericho was young and reckless. Braith felt it was too risky to send a prince into enemy territory, but Jericho insisted on going and doing something for their cause. Jericho meant to prove he was something more than the youngest son.

Their father was all too happy to send him. He was eager to see what Jericho might learn about the rebel faction, and hadn't cared if he lost his youngest. He had two other sons after all.

Jericho was the only member of their family Braith had been close to, and he hadn't wanted to lose him. However, his protests that if Jericho was captured, he could be used as a weapon against them had fallen on deaf ears. His father had made it very clear he wouldn't rescue Jericho if something went wrong.

Now Jericho was back, and if he'd returned that meant he'd discovered a way to bring down the rebel faction and destroy their enemies. Braith wasn't entirely sure he wanted to hear what it was.

BRAITH STOOD in his father's chambers with his hands folded over the head of his cane as he held it before him. It had been years since Braith entered his father's private living area. He couldn't see them now, but he knew that over the years his father had acquired more things, and amassed his fortune within these walls. He could feel those things pressing against him.

Keegan rested against his leg as he sat at his side. The wolf hated being around the king as much as Braith did.

"Your brother has returned," his father stated.

"So I've been told," Braith replied.

Braith didn't have to see his father to know he was a large and imposing figure. He was also sadistic. His father ruled with an iron fist; no one stepped out of line, and anyone who disobeyed was killed outright or placed in his father's trophy room.

Death did not come quickly to those offenders; they were tortured or destroyed in the most brutal ways possible to deter others who might try to bring down the king. He ruled by fear, and he had led them to victory in the war. The vampires respected and obeyed him for those reasons alone.

Braith felt he should respect him too, he was his father, and he had succeeded where many failed, but Braith felt nothing for the man except intense loathing.

Beatings were a near daily occurrence while growing up. Being the firstborn, Braith received the blunt force of them, and being the youngest boy Jericho was also heavily focused on. Caleb mainly managed to slip through unscathed. Caleb also had a malicious way about him their father recognized and admired.

By the time Jericho was born, Braith was nearly grown and almost untouchable, and his father eagerly turned his attention to a new target. It was why Braith had always felt closer to Jericho, looked out for his little brother, and hadn't liked it when he was sent straight into the lion's den.

It surprised Braith when his father hadn't destroyed him after he lost his vision; it was only the fact he'd adapted so well to being blind that he was allowed to live.Braith had honed his other senses to the point he could still fight as well as when he'd been able to see his attackers, and he was as ruthless as ever.

He wasn't like his father and Caleb though; he was not vicious for the pleasure of merely being vicious. He was a murderer when it was essential, and nothing more. He didn't relish in cruelty and torturing people, especially not children as his father and brother did.

"He has some interesting information for us," his father stated.

"Does he now?"

"Yes, I have called him and Caleb here."

"This is not a celebration announcement for the banquet then?"

"The banquet is not a celebration."

Braith kept his face impassive; he didn't want his father to see his curiosity was piqued. He turned at the sound of the door opening and listened to the footsteps thudding on the marble floor.

He recognized Caleb's footsteps leading the way, and behind him were Jericho's lighter steps. Caleb moved past him, but Jericho stopped before him. His hand clasped Braith's, as his other hand rested on his arm.

Braith accepted Jericho's hand, squeezing it affectionately within his. When Jericho left here, his hands were those of a boy. Now his callused hands were firm and strong. His grip was like a steel vise.

"You've grown," Braith said.

Braith could almost feel the cheerful demeanor Jericho radiated. He'd always been the easiest going of them all, the least affected by their world, and it seemed as if he was still the same.

But beneath it all, Braith sensed a tension and maturity in his brother that wasn't there when he left six years ago. They held hands for a long moment. Braith tried to size up the man before him; he had a feeling there were a lot of things he no longer knew about his little brother and may never know.

"I finally reached maturity," Jericho said.

Braith chuckled, but there was no humor in it. They'd always joked Jericho would never grow up, that he would be a thousand and still act like a seventeen-year-old. Braith thought it would be true, but he realized how wrong they'd both been.

Whatever happened to Jericho in the last six years, it changed him profoundly. This realization surprisingly saddened Braith. He'd missed his brother's camaraderie over the past years, and he realized he wouldn't be getting it back.

"I can tell," Braith said.

Jericho squeezed his hand again before releasing it.

"Tell your brothers what you told me," their father commanded.

Jericho took a few steps away from Braith before speaking. "After a year of living in the woods, fighting amongst the rebels, hiding my true nature, and struggling to earn their trust, I finally broke through part of their tight-knit, tight-lipped, group."

"How?" Caleb asked.

"I saved the life of a child who happened to be a cousin of the man leading the rebel faction. The child's parents started to trust me, accepted me, but it was still another year before the father took me to meet his cousin. I was blindfolded for this journey, and it was in the middle of the woods, but I met the man who leads the rebels. His name is David, I don't know his last name, most rebels have forsaken them, but I would recognize him if I saw him again."

"And you know where he lives?" Caleb inquired eagerly, the bloodlust evident in his voice.

"No one outside of family knows where David lives."

"Then what good is any of this?" Caleb hissed. "A man

named David leads these imbeciles. Six years and that's all you came up with?"

"Enough!" their father snapped. "Let your brother continue."

"As I was saying," Jericho grated through clenched teeth; his annoyance at being cut off and degraded more than apparent. At one time, Jericho would have laughed off Caleb's impatience.

"I met David, and though I don't know where he lives, I *do* know his family," Jericho said. "They may keep their living quarters a secret, but they all work together, especially David and his oldest son. In the beginning, I only knew the eldest son who is his second in command, but three years ago David's younger son became more involved, as did his daughter. Though they try to keep the girl out of most of the fighting, she is well trained, and a skilled hunter. She often went on food gathering trips, and would aid in planning and executing the raids as she knows the forest better than anyone."

Braith felt a knot forming in his stomach as uneasiness curdled through him. Arianna had been hunting for food when she was captured; she admitted as much. She'd said Max was caught because of her, that he could have run, but sacrificed himself in the hope he would be able to free her from captivity.

There were only two reasons a man would do that, either for love of the woman, or love of his leader. He'd assumed Max aspired to save her because they were friends, and he loved her, and because of his friendship with her brother.

He realized he might have been wrong; Max may have gone after her because he knew who she was, and who her father was. Because Max realized what a threat it was to their cause if one of the children of their leader was caught, discovered, and held by the enemy.

What kind of a mess had he gotten himself into with her?

"Okay, so the girl is a heathen and aspires to be a man," Caleb said. "So what?"

"Shut up, Caleb," Jericho grated.

Braith felt Caleb's disbelief ripple through him. He supposed he would have felt the same if he wasn't already terrified of what else Jericho might reveal.

"The *heathen* is also in our possession right now, or at least she was," Jericho said. "There was a raid on an outer encampment a few weeks ago; blood slaves were taken. At first, there were only rumors about exactly who was caught, but one child claimed a girl saved him. A girl who very much resembled David's daughter. No one knew anything for certain though, until last week."

Oh hell, Braith thought with an inward groan. Arianna had spoken of going back to rescue a child. His hand constricted on his cane as he fought the urge to flee back to his room and demand answers from her. Answers he feared receiving right now.

"And what happened last week?" Braith wanted to know.

"David's daughter didn't return as scheduled, and neither did one of his higher ranking lieutenants. It was confirmed the girl was taken. It hasn't been confirmed if she's alive as a blood slave, or not. That's why I risked blowing my cover to come back here," Jericho said.

"What good is any of this information?" Caleb inquired, but the irritation was gone from his voice.

"Humans tend to be attached to their children; so, if David's daughter is alive, and being kept as a blood slave, then we can use her as a weapon against him. He won't like the thought of his child treated in such a way, he will try to get her back, and he will be reckless. If she *is* dead, then we will have to dig up a blood slave who looks like her and try to use that girl against him. Either way, we have strong leverage over the rebels right now," Jericho explained.

"I want all of the blood slaves from the past few weeks

brought forth tonight for the banquet, Jericho will inspect them all," their father commanded.

Sensing Braith's growing concern, Keegan rose to pace around his feet.

"Perhaps it is your blood slave, Braith," Caleb taunted.

"Perhaps," he managed to agree.

"You have taken a blood slave?" Jericho's astonishment was evident in his voice.

"Yes, Braith has finally sunk to the levels of depravity the rest of us have enjoyed all these years. He did well for a blind man; she's a pretty little thing if you like redheads. Which, I do."

Braith was close to ripping the head off his cane as he anxiously waited for Jericho's response. If David's child were a redhead, they would all know shortly, and they would be racing up to his apartment to get at Arianna. They would use her and torture her before they killed her. Braith didn't know how he would stop them, but he was damn sure going to try.

Jericho released a mellifluous laugh. "No, fortunately for Braith's newest addition, David's daughter is not a redhead."

Relief coiled through him, but the tension in his chest still didn't ease. Something felt off about all of this. He itched to return to Arianna and question her, but he had a feeling that no matter how much had passed between them lately, she still wouldn't tell him about her family, especially if this David fellow was her father. He couldn't blame her for that; her family was probably far closer than his. Humans tended to cling to their loved ones.

If David was her father though, then why would Jericho lie about her hair color? Maybe he didn't consider her dark tresses red, but Braith doubted that.

Maybe he'd never actually seen the girl, but why would he lie about it? What did he have to gain by coming here and lying about any of this? Unless Jericho wanted to escape the woods and this was his excuse to return to the luxurious lifestyle he left behind.

That didn't seem right either, but he couldn't quite figure out this puzzle, not yet anyway. He knew he had to get back to Arianna, and he had to keep her away from Jericho. She couldn't go to the banquet tonight.

"Well, if she's not a redhead, then I'll be leaving my blood slave behind tonight. I'd prefer to mingle amongst the crowd, alone," Braith said.

"Already tired of your treat?" Caleb goaded. "Funny, but it didn't seem that way when I stumbled upon you earlier."

"A change is always good," Braith replied blandly.

"So be it," their father interjected. "I still require Jericho to see the girl, just in case."

"Of course," Braith murmured while struggling to remain calm. "Whenever you wish to stop by, Jericho. I will join the rest of you later."

Braith strode swiftly from the room with Keegan following at his side. It took everything he had not to break into a run and race back to Arianna.

CHAPTER THIRTEEN

Aria stood silently as Maggie slipped the beautiful dress over her head and began to tighten the strings running up the back of it. Aria stared at the shimmering green material, awed by the striking color as it flowed gracefully to the floor.

There were only two things she didn't like about the dress; its low cut revealed far too much of her cleavage than she was comfortable with, and the strings, that even now were cutting off her breath as they pressed against her still tender ribs.

"Is it too tight?" Maggie asked.

"A little," she admitted.

"I can loosen it, but it has to be snug to stay up. The prince chose this dress, but maybe he'd allow you to wear another if he knew it was hurting you."

Aria closed her eyes as she shook her head. She had to stay with this dress; no one could think Braith was offering any sympathy to her. If this were the dress he'd chosen, then she would wear it. There were probably already questions about them; she couldn't allow any more to be raised.

"No, it will be fine, and the prince won't allow me to change if this was his pick," Aria said.

"I'm sure he might; he probably wasn't thinking when he picked it. Men don't understand strings after all."

"It will be fine," Aria murmured.

Maggie sighed in aggravation but returned to pulling strings again. Aria clenched her teeth and strained to keep her face impassive as Maggie tried to be as gentle as she could.

"Do blood slaves often attend the banquets?" Aria asked, more to distract herself from the pain than out of any real sense of curiosity.

Maggie shrugged absently, but she looked a little troubled. "Not normally, and not when it is such a big celebration."

"What are they celebrating?" Aria inquired. She hadn't seen Braith since he sent her to his room, but Maggie had appeared shortly after.

"The youngest prince's return."

"Return from where?" Aria asked in surprise. She hadn't known he wasn't here; Braith had never mentioned it.

"No one knows, but he's been gone for six years."

"Odd," Aria whispered, mulling over Maggie's words.

"It's been speculated and whispered about for years." Maggie's voice was eager; she obviously enjoyed sharing the gossip. "Some say he left to aid the soldiers fighting against the rebellion, and others say he left for the love of a woman his father didn't approve of. Of course, no one liked that theory."

"Why not?"

Maggie was silent for a moment; her gaze darted around before she bent closer to Aria. "The young prince is *very* handsome. No one liked the idea of him with another woman. They all hoped they would snag him."

"Oh," Aria said dully. "I see."

However, she didn't see how anyone could be more handsome than Braith. She also didn't care to think about the women running around here trying to snag a prince for themselves, especially when it could never be her doing the snagging.

Aria closed her eyes as her ribs screamed in protest. She was so focused on trying to ignore the throbbing of her ribs that she didn't hear Braith arrive until he growled a command, "Leave us."

Aria's eyes flew open; her heart leapt when she spotted him standing in the doorway. He was magnificent, but he seemed unreasonably irritated and tense right now. Aria stood as Maggie glanced between them. She seemed hesitant to leave Aria by herself, but when Braith barked at her again, she scurried from the room.

A small tremor worked its way through Aria; she'd never seen Braith look like this, not even after she slapped him. The strange mix of anger and apprehension clinging to him left her breathless.

"What's wrong?" she whispered.

"If I'm going to keep you safe, then I must know more about you. Do you understand me, Arianna?" he asked. "There can be no secrets."

Her gaze darted nervously behind him. She could see little of the rooms beyond as his shoulders nearly took up the entire doorframe. "I don't understand, Braith; what is this about? What happened?"

"My youngest brother has returned."

"I heard."

He stalked unhurriedly forward, his body taut, and his jaw clenched as he surveyed her.

"Is he okay? Is everything all right?" she gushed out.

She was uncertain as to what was going on and why the return of his brother would cause such a strange reaction in him. She would be thrilled to see William and Daniel again, not looking as if she'd like to rip the head off something.

Perhaps the youngest brother was as revolting as the middle one.

"He's fine, Arianna, but he came back in search of someone," Braith said.

Aria's heart sputtered as a cold chill crept down her spine. She could only assume it was *her* he was probably looking for. But how was that possible? How would he know who she was? Until her capture, and Braith, the only vampires she encountered were killed.

"I don't understand," she whispered.

"Don't you?" he inquired.

Aria shook her head. She tried hard not to seem frightened, but she knew she was failing miserably. No matter how much she fought it, she could feel the horror showing on her face.

Then, a flicker of movement behind his back caught her attention. Her eyes widened, terror coursed through her as adrenaline slammed into her veins. She could only gape in silent dismay as the man behind Braith strode toward them.

Her mind couldn't comprehend what her eyes were seeing. It was impossible. What she was seeing was utterly *impossible!*

The overwhelming urge to flee was beginning to consume her. She didn't know what to say, or what to do.

She was trapped, cornered within these rooms with two vampires; one of which she was troubled she might be falling in love with. The other was a man she once trusted with her life, but who most likely came here to end it.

She tried to breathe, but the dress and her panic were making the simple task exceptionally difficult right now.

And then, she gave in to her instinctual urges.

Braith's loud curse followed her as she darted through the door of his bedroom, flew over the top of his bed, and raced for the entrance to the library. She didn't look back, didn't hesitate in her heedless rush. She didn't stop to think about where she could be going as she fled through the library.

She didn't kid herself into thinking she could escape, part of the reason they'd lost the war was that vampires were exceedingly fast, powerful, and so *damn* tough to kill.

But she had to try at least; she wasn't going down without a fight; she meant to stay alive for a few minutes more. She wished she had the stake to defend herself with, but it was tucked under the mattress and probably wouldn't do her much good anyway. It would have been something though.

As she ran, she threw things behind her. She tossed a chair here and an end table there, in an attempt to knock them off their pursuit. She wasn't entirely sure they were still behind her until she heard a reassuring grunt of pain as a piece of furniture made contact with one of her intended targets.

She grabbed the library door, slamming it shut behind her as she leapt forward. Out of the corner of her eye, she caught a rushing blur coming at her. Aria ducked low and darted to the side as the blur lunged at her.

A small yelp escaped when a hand skimmed over her back, but when she dove forward, she barely managed to escape its seeking grasp. It wasn't Braith who lunged at her; she would know his touch anywhere, but rather his brother, the *traitor*.

Her ribs screamed in protest, but they didn't slow her as fear for her life outweighed the agony. Scrambling back to her feet, she lifted the annoying hindrance of her dress as she leapt onto one of the sofas and jumped over the back of it in a fluid motion.

A frustrated shout sounded behind her, but she ignored it as she bounded forward. The door was just feet away.

For the first time since the chase started, true hope bloomed in her chest and excitement pounded through her. She'd managed to avoid two mature vampires in an enclosed space; surely, she would escape this never-ending nightmare.

Her fingers scrambled over the door as she worked hastily through the bolts that had been thrown. Those locks were rarely ever in place, as she'd learned earlier when Caleb walked in on them.

Locks, she realized that Braith's *brother* had turned into place. The door was almost open a foot when a hand slammed into it, banging it shut with a resounding crash that echoed throughout the room. She tugged uselessly on the handle for a few seconds, feeling like a fool as despair filled her.

She almost screamed for help, but there would be no one to come to her aid. No one to save her, she was trapped, and she'd been *discovered*. There was no escaping that fact. Not with Jack here now.

Except, his name wasn't Jack, was it? No, it was Jericho, and he wasn't one of her allies, but a member of the *royal* family. He'd come here to root her out, hand her over, and use her as a weapon against her family.

Well, the joke was on him then, wasn't it?

Because no matter what they did to her, her family wouldn't come here. It would be a suicide mission, and they knew it. There were far more lives at stake than just hers. She was willing to accept there would be no rescue mission. She only wished it hadn't come to this.

The sting of betrayal was sharp; she'd liked Jack, she'd trusted him and enjoyed spending time with him. She'd learned from him, and in return taught him a few tricks of her own.

Her father also liked and trusted the man. And the entire time Jack, no *Jericho*, had planned to betray him. Her body trembled from the bitterness radiating through her.

A hand wrapped around her waist, pulling her against a rigid body she recognized instantly as Braith's. She remained wooden within his grasp. She didn't try to kid herself, they'd grown close, she believed he might even care for her, but his loyalty would always be to his family and his kind.

He couldn't protect her from this, even if he chose to, which she wasn't sure he would. She was his enemy after all, and she had kept her true identity from him.

Her feet swung out when he spun her away from the door to face Jack.

Maggie was right, Jack was handsome, though Aria didn't think him as attractive as Braith. He was as tall as Braith, with a slightly leaner, more whipcord build. His hair, lightened by his time in the sun, wasn't as dark as Braith's but had streaks of brown and gold highlighting it.

His eyes were steel gray and severe when his gaze locked on hers. She glared ferociously back at him, resentment curling through her. She'd stab him right now if she had the stake, and she wouldn't think twice about it.

"I take it you two know each other," Braith grated, his voice low in her ear.

Aria clamped her jaw shut, resisting the urge to swing her feet back and kick him in the shin. Pissing him off right now would do her little good though.

"Is she who you're looking for?" Braith demanded harshly.

Aria remained unmoving in his grasp; her hands fisted as she stared fiercely at Jack/Jericho, her new greatest enemy. His eyes remained narrowed on her as he took her in.

"One of you answer me!" Braith snarled, shaking her a little within his grasp.

"Put me down!" she snapped.

His grip tightened on her. The frustration simmering in her raced toward a boiling point as everything inside her threatened to explode. She wanted to scream, wanted to kick and claw and go wild, but she did none of those things. She wouldn't give them the satisfaction of seeing her broken. She folded her arms over her chest as she focused her gaze stubbornly beyond Jack.

Seeming to realize she wasn't going to bend, Braith placed her down but didn't release her. He kept his arm latched around her waist.

"My family won't come for me," Aria declared. "No matter what happens, no matter what is done to me, they will *not* come for me. They can't."

Braith's fingers clutched on her stomach as he pressed her back flat against him. Astonishment filtered over Jack's face as he surveyed her and Braith.

"Damn it, Arianna! You should have told me!" Braith roared, causing her to flinch in response.

She shuddered, wishing she could take solace in his arms like she had before, but there was no solace to be found this time. Telling him wouldn't have changed any of this; it only would have denied her the few moments of happiness she'd found with him.

No matter what, she wouldn't trade those moments for anything, not even to avoid this. He couldn't protect her from this; he couldn't stop his family from torturing her, not once his brother revealed who she truly was. She didn't pretend to kid herself he could; it would be impossible.

Aria closed her eyes against the hot wash of tears filling them.

"I can't let you turn her in, Jericho."

Braith's words caused her eyes to fly open in shock. She trembled in his grasp, uncertain she'd heard him right. He released her to push her behind him and pin her against the door.

"I can't let you tell them it's her," Braith stated.

Amazement radiated from Jack as his gaze darted between them. "What are you saying?" he demanded.

"I'm saying you won't leave this room until we figure out

something, but it will not involve you taking her, and it will not involve you telling them who she is."

Aria rested her fingers on Braith's back, too taken aback to move for a second. Slowly, she peered around his back to look at Jack.

"Braith—" Jack started.

"You may be mature now, but I can still take you," Braith warned.

Aria gaped in astonishment; Jack's mouth dropped as his dark eyebrows shot into his hairline.

"Braith," she breathed. Her fingers curled into the shirt he wore; it awed her he was willing to protect her. He was going against his kind, going against his *family*, for *her*.

"She can't stay here, Braith," Jack retorted. "You know that."

"You're not giving her to them!" Braith took a threatening step toward his brother.

Aria jerked on his shirt. His body quivered with rage. She didn't want to die, didn't want to be handed over to be tortured and used against her family, but she also wasn't going to watch two brothers fight because of her. If Braith were injured, she would never forgive herself.

"I never planned to," Jack told him.

Both Aria and Braith started at his words.

"Excuse me?" Braith grated.

Jack rocked on his heels as he studied the two of them. "Apparently, we have a lot to discuss, but you can rest assured I'm not here to turn Aria over to our father."

"Then what are you here for?" Aria whispered.

Jack's eyes were remorseless when they met hers. "To bring you home."

Aria's fingers dug into Braith's shirt as she trembled against him; she was thrilled by Jack's words. Home! To be home in her forest, with her friends, and her *family*! To be free, running wild, back in the world she knew and loved so much, to be amongst the animals and trees, to breathe fresh air and not be leashed to do so. It was all so wonderful, and she craved it so badly she could almost taste it.

Then Braith turned toward her. She felt the heat of his gaze behind his glasses and the alarm filling him as she tilted her head back. She knew she couldn't keep the hope from her gaze, but a new sense of longing swirled within her. She would have her freedom, but she would not have *him*. She clung to him, unable to stop the surge of anguish shooting through her.

What was wrong with her?

She should embrace this; she should be halfway out the door with Jack right now, not standing here feeling confused and heartbroken. Her head dropped against his chest; she could scarcely breathe through the loss swamping her.

She barely knew him but there was so much between them, so much that would keep them apart, yet the idea of separating from him was almost unbearable. He remained unmoving for a moment before his hand slid into her hair and he cradled her against him.

"Yes," Braith agreed. "Apparently we *do* have a lot to discuss."

CHAPTER FOURTEEN

Braith didn't move away from the door; he didn't let Arianna step away from him either. He wasn't going to let her anywhere near Jericho, or Jericho anywhere near the door until he felt he could trust his brother, which might never happen.

"What happened here?" Jericho inquired.

"I might ask you the same question," Braith retorted sharply.

Jericho's gray eyes shone with merriment for a moment before they grew serious and harsh once more. Braith was right; his brother had matured. Jericho's demeanor was always carefree and lively, but it wasn't now.

Jericho looked perplexed and more than a little upset. He was thinner in the face, and in his build, most likely from not having access to the unlimited sustenance he'd enjoyed within the palace.

Although he was thinner, the muscles cording his body hadn't been there before. A jagged scar marred his cheek, it was fresh though, and with time it would disappear. Just as in another fifty years, Braith wouldn't have scars around his eyes anymore. It was only because of the severe amount of damage done to his eyes that the scars remained. He was still uncertain if he would ever fully regain his eyesight when he wasn't in Arianna's presence.

"What are you doing, Braith? If they discover this, they'll kill her. Father might even kill *you*."

Arianna's fingers tensed on his shirt.

"And you plan on what, just walking out of here with her?" Braith asked. "Do you believe father would allow that? And if someone else had claimed her, then what Jericho, were you going to kill them to free her?"

"I have a plan."

"And it doesn't risk her life at all?" Braith growled.

Jericho's gaze drifted toward Arianna. "There is always a risk, in everything we do. However, we felt the risk far outweighed the danger, if it meant getting Aria back."

"You followed me up here after Caleb told you she was a redhead, were you going to kill me?"

Jericho shifted uneasily. "No. I was sent here to find out if Aria was even still alive, and to see if I could get her safely out without jeopardizing either of our lives."

"And if you couldn't?"

"Then I was to leave."

Braith was somewhat put off by this statement. It made little sense to him, and he didn't entirely believe it. "They sent you in here just to have you leave if you couldn't do anything?"

"Jack worked his way up in our ranks; my father thinks very highly of him, he wouldn't risk losing him. Especially if he feels he can trust him." Arianna's gaze remained wary as she surveyed his brother.

"Is that so, *Jack*?" Braith inquired sharply.

Jericho shrugged as he reached into the pocket of his coat. "I couldn't give the rebels my real name, now could I? They may not know much about the royal family, or at least a lot of them don't, but I wasn't going to chance one of them possibly recognizing my name. And Jack is just less pretentious, don't you think?" He pulled something from his coat pocket and stepped toward them. "Your father instructed me to give you this."

Braith shifted, blocking her with his body as Jericho approached them. He snatched the thing from Jericho's hand, a low rumble of warning issued from him when Jericho went to take another step toward her.

At one point in time, Jericho had been the only one he trusted, that wasn't so now. Not when Arianna's life was on the line. He didn't want to kill his brother, but he would do what was necessary to keep her safe. Jericho appeared startled as he retreated from them.

Arianna held out her hand, accepting the small silver pendant Braith gave her. Her mouth parted as she stared down at it with tears in her eyes. "He gave this to you?" she whispered.

"So you would know you could trust me, that I was telling the truth. Your father trusts me, Aria, and you must trust me too."

Her fingers trembled as she stroked the silver horse head. Her eyes came up to Braith's; a single tear slipped free as she spoke. "It was my mother's; he would never give it to anyone he didn't trust."

Braith wiped the tear from her cheek; his hands enfolded hers as he turned his attention back to his brother. "And can he trust you?" Braith challenged.

"There are many things you don't know about me, Braith, many things you have never known," Jericho informed him.

"I can see that, but can he trust you, can *I* trust you?"

Jericho nodded. "If you desire her safety as much as her father and I do, then yes, you can trust me."

Braith studied him carefully, not at all convinced by his words. "What was supposed to happen if you couldn't get her, or yourself, out of here safely?"

Jericho's eyes were grave when he leaned back and folded his hands behind him. "If I am unable to get us both to safety, I am to leave so David can come here."

"Excuse me?" Arianna asked sharply; her head snapped up at Jericho's words.

Jericho's shoulders slumped as he ran his hand through his hair. "He's not going to risk losing us both. If I couldn't get you free, then I was to return to the woods, and he was going to offer himself in trade for you."

Arianna's breath hissed out of her; her hands clenched around the pendant. "That's crazy! Why would he do such a thing!?"

"Because he loves you; because you are his child. Because he would rather give his own life than think of you as a blood slave for the rest of yours."

Arianna shook her head rapidly. "No, he can't do that! There are thousands of other lives depending on him. Mine is nothing compared to that. *Nothing*! He knows better than to do something so foolish!"

Jericho studied her silently. Braith was unable to wrap his mind around the words Jericho uttered. A father who would give his life for his child... it was unfathomable to him.

He stared at Arianna's countenance, noting the stubborn set of her jaw, and the fire in her bright eyes. There was a rod of strength and courage running through her that was both admirable and slightly frightening. She was reckless, a danger to herself, and she had to be protected from the cruelty of the world. To give *his* life for her didn't seem so unbelievably farfetched. It was a strange realization, one he'd never experienced before, and never expected to experience.

For her, he could and would do anything. Even see.

That truth slammed into his gut as his hands tightened around hers. He felt that was the reason why he could see when he was near her. Something inside of him had somehow recognized her spirit as belonging to him. And then, because he wanted to see the face behind the bright spirit so badly, his eyes finally worked enough to see her on the stage. He would *always* be able to see her; he would always be able to find her.

"Of course, he knows better," Jericho agreed. "But he doesn't care, not when it comes to you. If I couldn't succeed in saving you, I was to try for Max and then retreat to the woods. Is Max still alive?"

"Yes," Arianna whispered, her voice choked with emotion.

"Katrina has him," Braith informed him.

Jericho nodded. "She might be difficult, but I'm sure I'll be able to get to him. Your father will not have to come for you."

"He was going to sacrifice himself for Max too?" she breathed.

Jericho shook his head. "No, your father cares for Max, and he is an important member of the rebellion, but he was not going to come for him. You are his daughter Aria, he loves you, and you are far more important to the rebellion than Max is."

Arianna shook her head forcefully at him. "No, I'm not!" she protested. "Max is a strong fighter, he rallies people to the cause, and he knows the woods as well as I do!"

"No one knows those woods as well as you do," Jericho muttered.

"It still makes no sense," she whispered.

"As your father's daughter, a man the rebels obviously admire and already follow, you would be able to rally the rebels to battle even more so than Max," Braith explained sympathetically.

Arianna bit her bottom lip; her gaze darted swiftly up to him. "I don't want this; I didn't want *any* of this."

She looked so lost, so frightened and sad. He'd never seen her like this; even dirty and bedraggled she'd displayed an admirable air of defiance. "I know, but it has to be dealt with."

She turned back to Jericho. "My father had to know it would be a suicide mission, and that they wouldn't release me, no matter what."

Jericho's gaze darted to Braith. "It was a chance he was willing to take if it meant he had the slightest possibility of saving your life. Daniel is capable of taking charge of the rebels within the camps, while William and I could lead the rebels outside the palace if your father had to come in here."

All the color drained rapidly from her face. "William?" she choked. "You brought *William* near here? What were you *thinking*, Jack? What was my *father* thinking?"

"He'll be fine," Jericho assured her.

"Fine?" she sputtered, releasing Braith as she took an angry step forward. "Are you trying to get him killed!?"

"Aria—"

"Don't you Aria me!" she retorted, suddenly charging at Jericho.

Braith was so thrown off by her sudden attack that he didn't spring into immediate action to try and stop her. She was in front of Jericho poking him relentlessly in the chest as he backed away from her. Her broken demeanor was gone, she radiated fury now.

"What were the *two* of you thinking?" she demanded.

Jericho seized her finger, keeping it within his grasp when she tried to pull it back. Arianna let out a raspy grunt of frustration, then wound up and kicked him as hard as she could in the shin. Jericho jumped back as Arianna glared at him.

"Damn it, Aria!" he barked at her.

"You're lucky I'm wearing this stupid dress and couldn't get my foot any higher!" she snapped back.

Jericho glared at her; she returned it wholeheartedly. Braith stepped forward and seized Jericho's arm. He didn't think his brother would harm her; in fact, Jericho seemed to like and admire her. There appeared to be an almost sibling-like connection between them, but Braith didn't want him touching her. He didn't like the idea of *any* other man touching her, even if it was his brother. Jericho glared at her for a moment longer before releasing her hand. Arianna looked as if she was going to kick him again, but she restrained herself.

"Now," Braith said coldly. "Who the hell is William?"

Arianna crossed her arms over her chest; displeasure radiated from her as she scowled ferociously. "My brother," she answered.

"Her *twin* brother," Jericho emphasized.

Braith didn't entirely understand why that seemed to upset her so much. "Okay," he said slowly.

Arianna finally turned her attention to Braith; the desperation in her eyes surprised him. "William and I are inseparable; we're rarely apart. The only reason he wasn't on the hunt with me that day was because he'd been wounded in a raid two days before. He's my twin; he's an extension of me just as I am of him. We're a lot alike."

"They're both hotheaded and reckless," Jericho explained further when Braith still didn't fully grasp what she was saying. "I blame it on the hair."

"You're an ass!" she snapped, spinning on her heel and storming away. "You and my father are *both* idiots! William won't stay away."

She strode rapidly to the door of the library where she stopped and stood uncertainly. Her arms wrapped around her stomach, she seemed torn, lost.

"That is why your father brought him."

She turned back at Jericho's words. "At least here your father can keep an eye on him and keep guards on him so he can't break free and do something that could get us all killed. If he left William behind, then he wouldn't be able to watch and monitor him."

Arianna's gaze flickered; then she bit her bottom lip and nodded. "You're right," she whispered.

Then she was moving again, coming back to Braith, slipping her hand into his. He didn't think she was aware she'd just sought him out for comfort, but he was pleased by the notion. She stared up at him for a moment, her eyes searching his face.

"What do we do?" she asked.

He didn't have an answer for her, but Jericho did. "Now, we make a plan to get you out of here."

Dismay filled Arianna's eyes; Braith felt a sharp twinge in his chest as his entire being recoiled at the idea. He knew she should leave, that she had to get somewhere safe, but he wasn't sure he could let her go to do so.

ARIA STARED NUMBLY out the window at the gardens; she hadn't moved from the window seat since Jack and Braith left to attend the banquet. They were both required to be there, but neither of them was willing to let her anywhere near it.

Braith didn't think Max would be brought, but he wasn't willing to take the chance. No one knew how Max was going to react when he saw Jack was one of the royal family; they didn't need her presence there to complicate things further.

The only problem was they hadn't settled anything before they left, and now she felt lost, confused, torn between her family and a man she was beginning to realize she loved. She didn't know when she started to love him; she supposed it was the night he comforted her after Lauren's attack. The revelation of his beautiful, wounded eyes had cemented it.

But what did that mean? Where did that leave her? Where did that leave *them*?

If she stayed here, she would forfeit her family, friends, and freedom forever. She would also have to die, probably sooner rather than later. If Aria left, she would be back with her loved ones, and in the life she cherished so much, but she would be leaving a big piece of herself behind. A piece she didn't think she would ever find again; in fact, Aria was sure she wouldn't.

She thought it should be an easy choice; her home, her life and her family, or a cruel and frightening life in a place she didn't understand. It wasn't even close to being easy though. Not when it meant she would never see Braith, or hold and feel him again.

That thought left her torn between freedom and a short, sweet life. She felt like crying, but she found tears wouldn't come. Her eyes were as dry and empty as a desert. She sat for hours, unable to move as the sweet sounds of music drifted up from below.

The sun had set a while ago; it was late when Braith returned. She hadn't realized she'd drifted off until she felt his arms wrapping around her. He lifted her smoothly from the window seat and cradled her against his chest as he carried her from the room.

"Braith?" she whispered, though she knew it was. She would know him anywhere.

"Go back to sleep, love."

She curled closer against his chest, thrilled by his words as his strength and scent captured her. Her fingers threaded inside his coat, pushing aside the buttons on his shirt. She rested her palm against his solid chest and somewhat cooler skin. She didn't think she'd ever get tired of touching him as her fingers slid over his skin.

He placed her gently on his bed and pressed a kiss against her forehead before he pulled reluctantly away from her. She watched through half closed eyes as he pulled his coat off, tossed it aside, and disappeared into the bathroom. She listened as he moved about, fighting against the deep pull of sleep threatening to claim her.

He was back again before she knew it with his hand on her shoulder. "Would you like me to remove your dress?"

Her mouth went dry; her heart leapt as apprehension and excitement tore through her. Sleep was officially forgotten in the face of his question. It was only then she realized Maggie hadn't returned. He must have told her to stay away for the night.

Would she like him to take off her dress? The relief to her ribs would be incredible, yet the intimacy of it terrified her.

She was wearing a slip beneath the dress, it was just as covering as the nightgowns, and she wanted the strings untied. And truth be told, she enjoyed the way he touched her. She swallowed before nodding. A smile flitted over his full mouth; it was so rare and fleeting it robbed her of her breath.

"So you have decided to reveal the stake to me?" he asked.

Her face drained of color. She'd completely forgotten about the stake, but after the events of this day, she hadn't felt safe without it. "You knew?" she accused.

That smile was back; if he made it just right the dimple would reappear. She might have found it adorable if his question hadn't so rocked her.

"I knew," he stated.

"How long have you known?"

"Since the beginning."

She glanced down at her chest, her eyebrows drawing together as she studied her cleavage. She'd spent a lot of time in front of the mirror making sure the stake was safely concealed.

Leaning over her, his scent of spices and something almost earthy engulfed her. The heat of his body warmed hers even as a chill lingered from his revelation. His lips were just centimeters from her cheek.

For a moment, she lost her train of thought as her need for him to touch and kiss her consumed her. Her fingers curled around his upper arms; she had to hold onto something to stay grounded in the sea of desire threatening to overwhelm her. His biceps flexed beneath her touch, his skin rippled over his solid muscles.

"I enjoy looking down there also," he murmured.

Her eyes flew wildly up to his. She thought she should feel outraged by his comment. Instead, her traitorous body was thrilled by it. "I...I don't even know what to say to that."

"That's a first."

Well, that sparked some anger from her. He chuckled, actually *chuckled*, as she glared at him. "Why did you let me keep it then?" she demanded.

He shrugged as he rested his hand on her waist. She completely forgot about being irritated with him as his presence overwhelmed her. Even through the fabric, she could feel the heat of his hand as it seared into her flesh. Her breasts tingled with anticipation as she instinctively pressed closer to him.

The pupils of his eyes dilated; his humor vanished as he focused on her mouth. Aria almost whimpered from the clamor surging through her body. His gaze focused on her lips before traveling over her body in a hungry perusal that left her feeling exposed and aching for something she didn't quite understand but instinctively knew he could help her with. Only he could ease this ache building within her.

"I planned to see what you would do with it," he said.

His eyes were back on hers as he leaned closer. Aria gulped, she almost pushed him away as she required some room to breathe, but she was mesmerized by him. Her hands curled around his arms; her thumb stroked the tantalizing flesh beneath the thin material of his shirt.

"I intended to use it against you," she said.

"I know."

"Then—"

"I was waiting to see what you would do. I was curious, but then if I'd known your true identity, I might have taken it from you a lot sooner."

She expected him to retreat at the reminder of who she was; instead, his lips brushed hers as he spoke. The feathery caress of every word caused her heart to thump against her ribs in response. It was tormenting, this touching, yet not touching. She wanted him to end it, wanted him to kiss her again, yet she found she enjoyed the sweet torture.

"You would have actually attempted to drive it through my heart?" he asked.

"In the beginning," she admitted. "And there's been a time or two I was tempted."

His laugh was low as it rumbled pleasantly out of his chest. "The feeling was mutual."

She couldn't help but grin at him. "I imagine it was. Though, I think I was far more tempted to stab Caleb than you." His amusement vanished so suddenly she gasped in surprise. "Braith—"

"I won't let him anywhere near you." His lips against hers were not teasing and playful anymore but compressed into a severe line.

"I... I didn't think you would," she stammered.

"Caleb is not like me or Jericho. He's the worst of everything bad about our species, and yours. I will make sure you're not exposed to him again."

"Is that why you send me away when he comes around?"

His muscles rippled beneath her hands; his lip curled into a small sneer. Aria's hands tightened around him as his eyes flashed red. She stared, astonished by the slip in his control and the blatant reminder of what he was and what he was capable of doing.

Trepidation trickled down her spine; she was unable to release him as she sensed something within him that had nothing to do with his hunger for her. For a brief moment, his vulnerability was exposed to her.

Her heart ached for the man beneath this hardened exterior, the one who wasn't like either of his brothers and most certainly wasn't like his hideously cruel father. The man who read to her, tended her injuries, and touched her with such tender reverence.

Love swelled within her; she almost cried from the force of the emotion growing within her chest until it encompassed her.

"I send you away so he won't see," Braith said.

"See what?"

"How much I need you. How much stronger you make me and how much your loss would destroy me."

When tears slid down her cheeks, he wiped them away with the pads of his thumbs. His fingers stroked her cheeks as a storm of emotion filled his eyes.

"What am I going to do with you, Arianna?" he breathed.

She shook her head; she had no answers for him, and there were none in this situation, not for them. She simply wanted to be with him, in this moment, and forget about everything trying to tear them apart. With a feathery touch, she ran the tips of her fingers over his full mouth. He shuddered in response, and his eyes darkened with desire.

"Let me get this thing off you," he said.

His hands were gentle on her as he slipped the ties of her

dress free, allowing her to breathe easily for the first time in hours as her aching ribs were finally freed.

"Why did you wear this thing with your ribs in the condition they are?" he muttered in annoyance.

"You chose it," she reminded him.

His forehead creased. "I didn't know it required these strings; I simply liked the color and thought it would look good on you. You could have said no."

She breathed slowly in and out as she relished the full air in her lungs. "Maggie suggested that, but I didn't think it would look right if I went against the dress you chose for me. Maggie's a nice girl, but I don't trust anyone in this place."

He cursed as he sat back and rested his hand on her arm. He was no longer looking at her, but staring into the dark. She knew he was wondering if it would be best for her to leave, and the thought terrified her. It *was* best if she left, for both of them, but it was the last thing she wanted to do.

His hand rubbed her arm before he lifted her effortlessly to her feet. Aria stared at him in surprise, her lips parted. His full mouth curved into a smile as he slid the dress down her, letting it pool on the ground at her feet. Her face flared with heat as she stepped out of the material.

The handle of the stake poked out from the thin undergarments still covering her. His fingers brushed tantalizingly against her skin as he plucked it free and stared at it for a moment. His eyes were gleaming with amusement as he wagged the stake before her.

"The nightstand leg?" he asked.

"Yeah."

"Destructive little human."

He held the stake for a moment more before snapping it in half between his thumb and index finger. Aria's mouth dropped at the display of strength. Granted, it wasn't the strongest stake, but he'd snapped it with barely a flick of his wrist. She knew vampires were powerful, but she had a feeling there was a wealth of strength and power within him she hadn't begun to see yet.

She imagined it was terrifying, and she hoped she never had to see it.

For the first time, she noticed his legs were bare, and he wore only a pair of shorts. Her mouth went dry, and her heart thumped with barely contained excitement. His thighs were corded; the muscles in them stood out sharply as he moved. Her pulse pounded as he unbuttoned his shirt and slid the material free.

She was gawking, she knew it, but she couldn't stop herself from taking in the perfectly sculpted muscles ridging his abdomen, broad shoulders, and chest. Dark hair ran across his chest, before tapering toward an area hidden by his shorts. Her face burned hotter as she realized she'd followed that trail of hair all the way down to where it vanished from view.

It seemed as if someone decided to create the perfect man and had come up with *him*. And he was staring at her from under hooded eyes that made her toes curl into the thick carpet.

Holy hell, she was in over her head. She had no experience with this. There were bare-chested men in the woods, she'd seen male legs before, but none of those chests or legs had this much of an overwhelming, dizzying effect on her. She felt like a child at the same time she became aware of herself as a woman.

"Arianna?"

She glanced at him from beneath lowered lashes as she struggled to control her embarrassment; she failed miserably. "My friends call me Aria," she said, for lack of anything else to say, or do.

His hand was gentle as it caressed her cheek, tilting her face, so she had to look at him. "We're a little more than friends, don't you think?" His voice was low and laced with passion.

There were no more words left in her; there was nothing she

could say to that because it was true. They were more than friends, and at that moment she would have done anything he asked of her. She stepped closer to him and, resting her hands on his bare chest, she marveled at the broad, well-muscled expanse as her fingers trailed over it.

He was unmoving beneath her touch while he let her explore him as she saw fit. She yearned to touch all of him, but her fingers froze on the ridges sculpting his abdomen, just above the line of his shorts.

He pulled her forward; kissing her forehead as he held her flush against him. "You're beautiful, Arianna."

She blinked in surprise. No one had ever said that to her, and though she knew it wasn't true, she couldn't stop the thrill of pleasure racing through her at his words. It seemed as if he'd meant it.

"No, Braith, but thank—"

"Yes, Arianna, to me, you're the most beautiful woman in the world."

Tears burned her eyes as she searched his gaze, but all she saw was honesty and desire radiating back at her. Her fingers curled against his skin as love bloomed rapidly through her chest.

She couldn't fight the tidal wave of emotion overtaking her. The burning in his gaze puzzled her as it was more than just sexual. Then, with sudden clarity, she knew what that look was. What he so desperately needed from her.

What he lacked that she could give to him.

"Did you feed tonight, Braith?" He shook his head; his eyes briefly closed as his thumb massaged her cheek. "Why not?"

"I cannot feed as often as I once did," he answered.

She frowned at him, confused by his words, and then realization swamped her. "Because if you did, they would question what you were doing with me. What use could I possibly be to you if you still need to feed on others?"

He didn't say anything, just looked beyond her at the back

170

wall. His jaw clenched as he grated his teeth. His hand trembled on her cheek before he slid it into her hair. "It's more than that, Arianna."

She tilted her chin back to drink in the sight of him. He was magnificent, powerful, and for now, in this moment, it was just the two of them. There was no blood slave and master; there was no Jack and Max. Even her forest and family didn't exist. It was just them, and they didn't have to worry or fear anything else, not here.

"What is it then?" she asked.

He bent closer until his mouth was just inches from hers. The hand entangled in her hair, pulled her head a little to the side. His other hand traced her pounding pulse. His finger lingered on her neck as his eyes dilated to near pinpoints of hunger.

"Yours is the only blood I've craved since I set eyes on you," he said. "Nothing else could completely satisfy me."

A sob caught in her throat. She could only stare at him in awe as he bent to place a kiss on her throat. His lips were gentle, but beneath them, she could feel the press of his fangs. He tried not to let her know they were there but she knew, and more than that, everything in her thrilled at the thought of them.

She should be terrified, should be repulsed by the mere thought of allowing him to feed on her, but it was all she could think about. It was *all* she desired.

Her blood pumped more vigorously, goose bumps broke out across her skin. Her hands curled against his corded muscles as he dropped smooth kisses across her neck, her cheek, before brushing briefly against her mouth.

Aria's knees trembled. She barely remained standing when his tongue flickered against her lips. Her mouth parted eagerly to his hungry invasion. His arm locked around her waist as he lifted her off her feet, keeping her pressed flush against him. Aria wrapped her arms around his neck, clinging to him as he laid her on the bed and leveled himself gradually on top of her.

The weight of him was wonderful; *everything* about him was wonderful.

She never wanted this moment to end. She wished she could freeze time, that she could simply lay here with him and enjoy the miracle of this moment. She wished they would never have to face the world or any of the horrible things in it again, but no matter what happened, she would enjoy this night.

They would have one moment of pure happiness and peace before the harsh reality they faced came crashing back.

His kiss became more urgent, fevered. She could feel the lust he radiated. Her head spun; her body was out of control as she held on to him, using him as an anchor in a suddenly turbulent world.

His hands moved over her in a whisper caress that caused her to tremble everywhere. His lips were on her neck, his teeth skimmed over her throat, but he didn't bite.

He wouldn't, she realized, unless she gave him permission.

She was close to tears when she turned her head to bury her face in his neck. She pressed her mouth against his solid flesh; clutching his arms as she tried to keep herself grounded though she knew it was impossible.

"It's okay," she breathed. "It's okay."

He didn't seem to hear her at first as he didn't stop kissing her neck. Then his arms locked around her and he drew slowly back from her. She pushed his dark locks aside as she traced the scars circling his eyes.

"Arianna?"

Her fingers moved over his cheekbones, then down to the curve of his full mouth. She trailed over his lips, but he recoiled when she touched his fangs.

"Don't," she pleaded, refusing to let him pull away from her.

His forehead furrowed in confusion, but he didn't move any further away from her. She was startled to realize the sensation of running her fingers over his pointed teeth was tantalizing and breathtaking.

Aria wasn't as frightened by it as she thought she would be, as she *should* be. He was far more powerful than her; he could easily kill her, yet there was no fear within her because it was *Braith*.

"It's okay," she said again, her fingers stilling on his teeth. "You're hungry, and I can ease that. *I* want this, Braith."

"Arianna." His voice was a low anguish filled moan as he dropped his head into the hollow of her neck. His shoulders shook beneath her; the tension in him was almost palpable. "You don't know what you're asking for."

"I'm asking for you."

His shaking increased; his hands stopped running over her as he cradled the back of her head. Her heart swelled further with love. Braith fought to restrain himself because he feared he might harm her, even though she was willingly offering him what he so desperately needed.

"It's okay," she said again.

She grasped the back of his head, gently turning it toward the hollow of her neck. Small tremors racked him as she pressed his extended fangs against her rapid pulse. "It's yours, Braith, *I'm* yours. Take it. Take *me*. I want to be the one that satisfies you, not them."

He groaned loudly. She felt the point where he lost control, and his craving for her took over. Aria gasped; her fingers dug sharply into his back as his lips pressed hotly against her flesh before skimming back to reveal his hard fangs. His tongue swirled over her neck before his teeth punctured her skin and struck deep into her vein.

For a moment, the entire world blurred; she could think of

nothing and see nothing except for him. He was everywhere, over her, in her, a part of her as his fangs sank into her completely.

Then, little by little, they became separate entities again. She could make out his hunger, his thirst, his fascination with her as he consumed her. He drank deeper than he ever had from anyone before. And somehow, though he didn't say it, she knew that was true.

His thoughts mingled at the edges of her conscious as his pleasure engulfed her. He craved all of her; he would *never* get enough of her, and she didn't want him to.

He pushed against her; the weight of his body pressed her more firmly into the mattress. A groan of ecstasy escaped her; her fingers convulsed on his back as he bit down sharply. She heard cartilage snap, *her* cartilage, but she didn't care. It didn't hurt; she didn't feel anything above the blood being pulled eagerly from her, and the ecstasy consuming them both.

She knew she should be frightened, knew this was going beyond either of their control, but she wasn't scared. As long as she was in his arms, she knew she would never be afraid again. Blood ran down her neck to stain the sheets beneath her, but she still didn't feel any alarm. Instead, love overflowed from her.

It wasn't until he growled low, and bit down harder, that she realized the words, *I love you,* were spilling from her in an unending chorus that she couldn't stop until a wave of blackness washed her away into nothingness.

While she drifted in and out of consciousness, pleasant memories rolled in like the rain before slipping away again. Dreams came and went; shadows spun through her mind. Braith was holding her, cradling her against his chest, whispering for her not to leave him, but she felt he should know she would never leave him. She tried to tell him so repeatedly.

He offered her something wet and a little sticky on his wrist.

She pushed him away, telling him he was enough, but he made her take his wrist into her mouth and begged her to swallow.

The warm, sweet liquid tasted of him, and she found herself unable to turn away from his offering. As she drank greedily, she thought she heard him whispering, *I love you*, but she couldn't be sure. Finally, she drifted into a state of profound bliss where she knew she was safe in his arms.

CHAPTER FIFTEEN

"Aria! Aria! Arianna!" She groaned in annoyance as she tried to roll away from the hands shaking her, but they refused to let go as they shook her again, this time more incessantly. "*Arianna!*"

She batted at the hands in an attempt to break free, but she was so tired, and they wouldn't let her go.

"Stop!" she protested.

"Get up, Aria, you have to get up!"

The urgency in the voice finally pierced through the haze of bliss and exhaustion enveloping her. She cracked open an eye and frowned at the blurry face before her. It was too much effort to concentrate on the face; instead, her eye drifted shut, and she snuggled deeper into the delightful bed beneath her.

The voice swore loudly; then, before she knew what was happening, she was heaved out of bed and tossed over someone's shoulder. She sputtered in disbelief as she was spun around in a circle before being dumped on the bed once more.

"Get up, Aria, or I'm going to throw you in a tub of cold water."

She blinked as she tried to clear her blurry vision. Eventually, her eyes focused; she frowned in indignation when Jack came into view. Then, reality crashed over her as she recalled where she was.

She gasped in horror; bolting upright in the bed, she pulled the comforter against her chest. She still wore the slip, but where she hadn't been embarrassed for Braith to see her in it, she was mortified Jack was.

"Jack!" she cried as she tried to process what was going on.

She was in Braith's bed, wasn't she? But where was Braith, and what was Jack doing here?

"Where's Braith?" she demanded.

Jack had turned away from her to search for something, but she didn't know what it was until a pile of clothes fell into her lap. She stared at the pants and cotton shirt in disbelief. They were similar to the clothes she'd worn in the woods, except these were pitch black instead of brown or green.

"He was called to an emergency meeting with our father," Jack said. "Get dressed. We have to go before he gets back."

"Wait! What?" she sputtered.

"We have to go, Aria! Now!" he snapped impatiently. "Get dressed."

Shock flooded her; her mind spun in confusion. Go? Now? Leave Braith? No, no she couldn't. Not after last night, she could *never* leave him after last night.

"No, Jack, no I can't."

"Aria—"

"No, you don't understand, Jack. I can't leave, I simply can't."

He seized her cheeks as he thrust his face into hers. She knew that look well; it was nearly identical to Braith's when he lost patience with her and was reaching a snapping point.

"*You* don't understand, Aria," he said. "This is our only chance at escape; if we don't leave now then you'll remain here, and your father will come for you, and he *will* die. Now get up, and get dressed."

She gaped at Jack, then at the clothes, then back at Jack. She couldn't leave Braith; she couldn't. She loved him! And though she wasn't entirely sure, she thought he might have said he loved her too last night.

But it was all so hazy, so distorted and confusing, and it was all so astonishing that she could barely contain her excitement over it. Until the awfulness of this situation came surging back to the forefront.

"Aria—"

"No, Jack, no. I'd like to stay. I can't leave him." Jack's eyes widened in surprise, the blue flecks in them were more clearly visible as he gazed at her. "Jack, please—"

"You cannot stay here, Aria. I can't let that happen. No matter what, your father will come after you."

"No." She seized Jack's hands. "Not if you tell him I'm dead."

"Max—"

"Tell Max the same thing."

Jack's jaw clenched, and his nostrils flared. He stared at her as if he didn't recognize her; stared at her as if he didn't have a clue who she was. And truth be told, she didn't know who she was anymore either. All she knew was her heart belonged to Braith, and she couldn't leave him.

"Max is here, Aria, he knows you're alive," Jack said. "He's keeping a lookout right now."

Her gaze darted around the room as she searched out Max, but she didn't see him anywhere. Disappointment filled her; she would like to see her friend again, at least once more to make sure he was okay.

"Then tell them I'm happy, Jack, because I am. I... I..." She broke off; her fingers clutched at the blanket. She heaved an irritated sigh before she turned back to Braith's brother. "I love him."

Jack sat back as he stared at her in consternation. "Aria—"

She seized his hand as she leaned forward. She was desperate for him to understand, desperate for him to hear and believe what she was saying. She knew what Jack was now, but she was surprised to realize she still trusted him, and he was the only one who could help her right now.

"I know it makes no sense, but I *do* love him, and I want to stay with him," she insisted.

Jack's gaze turned pitying; sadness crept over his features as he shook his head. "Aria—"

"Please, Jack, I—"

His hands cradled her cheeks. "He has a fiancée, Aria."

Her words broke off, sputtered, and died. Dismay surged through her, she couldn't breathe, couldn't move. She could only sit there and stare at him, her mouth open, and her heart shattering as something within her curdled and died.

"No, not possible, he... No," she said.

"*Yes*, Aria. They've been betrothed for over a year. They're getting married in six months."

Suddenly she was choking on the air she struggled to get into her lungs. The strange, guttural sounds coming from her didn't sound human to her. She didn't feel human anymore as her heart shredded and a moan of agony died within her. Jack held her as she rocked forward, unable to fully comprehend his words, unable to function through the agonizing grief consuming her.

"I'm sorry, Aria. I am so sorry, but you can't stay here. She'll have you killed as soon as the wedding is over, and he won't be able to save you. He's my brother, but he will never go against my father. It's the curse of the firstborn, I suppose, to be the one reared to one day rule, to do what is expected, and to bear the heavy burdens of duty. You and I both know Braith is not the same bastard my father is, and the kingdom won't be the same under his rule."

Maybe she'd known that yesterday, maybe yesterday she would have said Braith would make a better king than his father, but now she didn't know anything at all. For all she knew, he'd been playing her all along, and she'd fallen for it.

"He cannot leave here, Aria; he'll do what is expected of him because he knows it's for the good of everyone involved. It's also why he'll go through with this marriage. Now, you have to pull yourself together because we have to get out of here."

He pulled her out of bed and stood her on shaking legs.

"Don't force me to dress you, Aria."

She shook her head as tears streamed down her cheeks and she grasped the clothes he thrust at her. She could only gaze dazedly at him. She hated the awful pity in his eyes, hated the fact she looked so weak and pathetic right now.

"We have to go; get dressed," he said.

Jack turned away. Her hands trembled as she pulled the slip over her head. The spectacle of her blood staining the neck of the nightgown almost made her vomit. He was engaged?

He was *engaged*!

They were the only words running through her head, the only thing she could focus on right now. He was engaged, and he never told her. He'd slept beside her, held her, and kissed her. He'd *fed* off of her. He used her, and all the while he knew he had a fiancée.

She never kidded herself with dreams of a future for them, but she'd never expected this betrayal. If he'd told her, she never would have allowed things to go this far. She sure as *hell* wouldn't have allowed him to feed on her.

Her trembling hands made it impossible for her to get the buttons together. Then, Jack was back before her.

"You let him feed on you," Jack stated.

Aria blinked at him as he hastily buttoned her shirt. She wasn't embarrassed Jack was seeing this much of her anymore;

nothing else could faze her. He grasped her shoulders, shaking her.

"Aria, you have to listen to me. You must concentrate on me for a moment; it's important."

She managed a nod, and she barely managed that.

"He fed on you."

It wasn't a question. It was quite obvious Braith had fed from her between the bloodstained slip and bed. She winced as Jack brushed at the blood on her neck, rubbing against the painful bite marking her.

"Did he give you any of his blood?" Jack asked.

"Excuse me?"

Jack was growing frustrated with her. "*Think* Aria! This is important! Did *you* feed on *him?*" He enunciated each word clearly and sharply.

Aria blinked as she tried to recall the night, but her mind and body shied away from the painful memories. It was too much. She couldn't think about it. It was all a lie. A cruel, brutal lie.

It meant so much to her, yet it had meant absolutely nothing to Braith. She was nothing but a blood slave after all. She didn't know why he'd waited so long to feed on her, and she didn't care to think about it.

There was no way she could figure out what he'd been thinking, or doing, or why. She wasn't cruel and manipulative like him; she would never understand why he'd done this to her.

It didn't matter anymore. It all meant nothing. For the first time in her life, she'd been a silly fool who let her defenses down, and she'd gotten what she always expected. Nothing.

"Aria!" Jack barked.

She blinked him into focus before shaking her head stubbornly. "No, I... No. What does it matter anyway?"

"It matters. Are you sure?"

She bit her bottom lip. There had been so many fantastic

dreams of peace and love and security. There had been a dream about something sweet and delicious tasting, but they'd been nothing more than dreams.

They couldn't have been anything more, Braith was engaged after all, and therefore he never would have told her he loved her. He already belonged to someone else. Dreams, nothing but awful, *shattered* dreams.

"No," she whispered. "No, I didn't."

Jack's shoulders slumped in relief as he nodded. "Good, good. We must go."

She didn't respond as he seized her arm. He pulled her through the library, the sitting room, and then into the bedroom she used upon first arriving. Max stood by an open doorway she'd never seen before. It seemed to have magically appeared in the wall next to the bed she'd slept in.

Max's eyes filled with love when he spotted her. For a moment, the sight of her friend was enough to make her forget her grief. A cry of happiness escaped as she raced forward and threw herself into his arms. He'd lost weight; his face was gaunt, his eyes far wiser and sadder, but his arms were still warm and secure as they wrapped around her.

"Later, later." Jack pushed them toward the open doorway, shoving them into a dark tunnel.

"What is this?" Aria demanded.

"Security tunnels; all the apartments have them. They lead out of the palace. We have to go fast though; they'll kill us if they find us, and personally, I don't feel like being caught and branded as a traitor. It's not a pleasant death," Jack informed her.

Aria imagined it probably wasn't. She stared around the dark, confining tunnel in disbelief. The entire time she searched for a way to escape, the route had been within her room. She'd *slept* right next to it. The realization only added insult to injury.

She kept her hand in Max's, taking strength in his warm

touch as she struggled not to cry while they fled through the dark tunnel with Jack leading the way. She could barely see through the darkness, but Jack moved with speed and unerring sureness of foot.

She didn't look back until they arrived at the end of the tunnel, and then she only paused for a moment. She vowed she'd never look back after this, never think about anything that had happened within those hated walls again. Though she desperately wanted it to be true, she knew she was lying to herself.

She stared down the darkened tunnel but didn't truly see it as tears caused it to blur before her. Her body throbbed with the force of the anguish consuming her. She was leaving that world behind, she would never return to it, but it would haunt her for the rest of her days.

She would never escape what happened within those walls, never be free of the torment Braith's betrayal had inflicted on her. She also knew the woman who walked out of this tunnel was far different than the girl who first entered the palace as a captive.

Max tugged on her hand, pulling her forward and tearing her from her melancholy thoughts. She would never look back again; especially not now that she had her freedom and would soon have her family. They plunged into the sanctuary of her beloved woods, blending seamlessly into the surrounding forest.

BRAITH SHOOK as fury boiled through his blood and caused his eternal darkness to turn a violent shade of red.

She was gone.

He'd known it the moment he stepped back into his apartment. He sensed her absence when he was downstairs, but it wasn't until he returned that the lack of her radiance confirmed his fear.

Keegan whimpered as he crept away from Braith's leg and slunk into the shattered debris littering the room. To say he'd lost his temper would be an understatement; he'd been in a rage, furious at himself, with Jericho, and with *her*.

He knew his youngest brother was behind this; no one else could have taken her from these rooms without being seen. There was no one else who would have known Braith hadn't been present, and the location of the tunnel within his apartment.

"Your Highness."

He turned at the sound of the wavering voice. His hands clenched on the head of his cane; it was essential now that he'd destroyed the room. There were obstacles in his way that weren't there before, and she was no longer present to light the darkness.

"There is no sign of them outside of the palace walls," the voice said.

"Of course there isn't," Braith sneered.

Jericho was smart, quick, and he would be far from here by now. Using his cane, Braith maneuvered his way through the shattered remains of his furniture. His display of temper and destruction could be blamed on the fact his brother stole his blood slave. All his kind would understand the betrayal, the insult to his pride, and the denial of his toy.

But as he stopped in the doorway of his bedroom, he knew it was far more than that.

The scent of her blood assailed him. It burned into his nostrils, flared through his body, and caused an aching hunger to explode through him. She'd been magnificent, free and giving last night, and so delectably satisfying. Her delicious blood had filled and nourished him in a way he'd never experienced before.

In fact, he was so swept away by it that he'd nearly destroyed them both.

He'd wanted her with him, forever; he'd been consumed with the compulsion to change her and have her for eternity. It was an insane idea, and thankfully he regained control of himself before he pushed her into a place few ever came back from. Very few humans survived the change.

He'd been so consumed by her that he nearly ended her life. In all his many years, he'd never been so careless or so out of control with his thirst.

But even more potent than her blood were her words. Whispered words of love repeated as she embraced him. Words he'd never heard before but relished and he'd believed them. Just as he'd believed her vow never to leave him, and to stay with him always.

Lies, it had all been lies, and he was the fool who believed them.

Now, he almost wished he'd killed her; almost wished he'd never given her the opportunity to betray him like this. He fought the urge to smash his cane off the wall. He wanted to rip his brother limb from limb; wanted to shake her and make her tell him why she'd offered her blood to him, why she said him she loved him and then left him the very next morning.

The betrayal made him the angriest; the betrayal made him yearn to hunt them down and destroy them. And he could, he could find her so easily.

He could track her through her precious woods, seize her, drag her back here, and lock her away for the rest of her miserable life. He could make her pay dearly for her betrayal—make his brother pay. He could make both of their lives a living hell if he chose to. He could destroy and ruin them completely.

Arianna may not have realized his blood in her veins made it so he could find her whenever he chose, but his brother should have known better. Jericho should have known Braith would come after them. He would make Jericho pay for helping her and make her pay for her lies.

"The other blood slave?" he demanded as he turned back to the servant.

He could hear the man shifting nervously and feel the panic coming from him. "Is also gone, your majesty."

Rage suffused him once more; he couldn't stop himself from smashing his cane off the wall. The impact jarred through his hand, shattered the cane, and sent pieces of debris flying. He wasn't sure if it was Keegan or the servant yelping in response. Braith stood for a moment, barely able to keep his fury under control.

"Get me a new cane," he snarled.

When the servant scrambled away, his feet cluttered over the debris. Braith stood for a while, trying to regain control of himself and his wildly swinging emotions. It was a while before he felt calm enough to move again without ripping something to shreds. It took even longer before he could take a new cane from the servant without being worried he might kill the innocent man.

"We'll go after them; we'll make them pay."

Braith turned at the sound of Caleb's voice. It was funny that just yesterday Jericho had been his favorite. Now, he despised him even more than he ever could have disliked Caleb.

"There are already men gathering to hunt them," Caleb said.

Braith could find her in a matter of hours, but he found himself remaining where he was. He didn't want that traitorous bitch back in his life, didn't *ever* want to see her again.

He preferred his world of blackness to the sight of her disloyal, hideous face. She wanted her freedom so badly she'd lied and manipulated for it; as far as he was concerned, she could have it. She could have her starvation and cold, her misery and dirt; she could have everything she craved.

He wanted nothing to do with her anymore, and wouldn't stand in her way.

"Jericho has been labeled a traitor," Caleb continued.

"He is," Braith growled.

"There is a large bounty on his head; it shouldn't be long before one of the starving masses turns him in. I am sure the other two slaves will be in his vicinity, and I'm also certain he will turn on them as swiftly as he turned on us when we find him."

Braith wrapped both his hands around the head of his new cane. "If he is found, he will be brought to me, alive. *All* of them are to be brought to me."

"Of course," Caleb murmured in assent.

Braith closed his eyes as he tried not to think about the depth of Arianna's betrayal. He wouldn't hunt them down; he wouldn't go into the woods after the two people he'd come to trust the most. But if they were captured and brought back here, he would be the one to make sure Jericho was destroyed, and he would be the one to hand Arianna over to Caleb.

Then, he would sit back and relish in the sounds of her screams as Caleb did what he did best.

Until then, he was going to gorge himself on as much blood as it took to help him forget this horrendous mess.

He moved toward Caleb, finally beginning to understand his brother's cruelty and hatred as those emotions took root in his gut, spread through his chest, and buried him beneath their crushing weight.

He'd never experienced these emotions to this degree before, never knew that it was possible to do so until now. But he relished in the hatred and bloodlust consuming him; they were the only things that helped to bury his betrayal and hurt.

"Clean up this mess," he barked at the servant.

Keegan padded after Braith, following him to the dungeons. The wolf had never been here; it had been years since Braith had been down here, mainly because he despised it.

Now, he found himself craving it, needing it, desiring it with a ferocity that left him shaken. When he threw the doors to the dungeons open, the scent of humans and dread assaulted him. These were the blood slaves of the royal family, at least until they were drained dry and discarded to make room for others.

He moved quickly through, stopping only briefly to pick out three women from behind the bars. He didn't know what they looked like, but the scent of their blood was not as repulsive to him as some of the others.

"Have them cleaned and brought to me," he commanded the guards.

He may not have Arianna now, but he would satisfy himself and attempt to ease some of his pulsating bloodlust.

It wasn't lost on him that a skinny wisp of a girl managed to do in one month what his father had failed for over nine hundred years to accomplish. She had succeeded in turning him into a coldhearted, bloodthirsty monster.

*

Turn the page for a sneak peek of *Renegade*, book 2 in The Captive series.

RENEGADE, THE CAPTIVE SERIES BOOK 2

ARIA DIDN'T HAVE to look up to know Max had arrived. He'd joined her here, at the same time every day for the last month. Even if she wasn't expecting him, she would have detected his presence by his subtle smell and quiet step.

He settled onto the ground beside her, remaining silent as he picked up a rock and leisurely skipped it across the lake. Aria handed him the fishing pole beside her; the hook was already baited and ready for him. He took it from her and cast it into the center of the lake.

Aria swung her feet back and forth, her toes skimming across the water. The cool water felt wonderful against her overheated skin. Using the back of her arm, she wiped away the sweat already beading on her forehead. They sat for a while together, wordlessly reeling in the fish they caught. They kept the good ones and tossed back the ones that were too small.

Aria had started retreating to this spot soon after her escape from being a blood slave and her subsequent return home. Max had found her here two days later. They rarely spoke, they didn't have to.

They had both been inside that place, both owned and used, and both forever marred by the vampires who had possessed them. The *monsters* who had held them. Though, decidedly, Max's experience was far worse than hers.

She had been owned, led around by a leash and used, but the extent of her use was her fault. She'd willingly given the prince her blood, mistakenly thinking she was falling in love with the deceptive bastard, but that was before she learned he was engaged.

Though she hated the prince now, she couldn't deny the sharp stab of sorrow that pierced her at the thought of him marrying another woman. It brought tears to her eyes every time it crossed her mind, which was far more often than she cared to admit.

But, no matter how badly she'd been hurt, no matter how betrayed she felt, her experience wasn't anywhere near as awful as Max's. Though they didn't talk about it, she knew what happened to blood slaves. They were used, abused, and discarded when their owners grew tired of them.

Max always wore long sleeves, but occasionally his shirt would ride up, and she would catch a glimpse of the marks and burns scarring his fair skin. She'd seen the haunted look filling his bright blue eyes when he didn't think anyone was looking.

She'd suffered abuse while within the palace, but it had been at the hands of a human servant and not the vampire prince. The prince broke her heart, but he never intentionally inflicted any bodily harm on her that she hadn't asked for. In fact, he had been unfailingly tender with her.

She hated to acknowledge it, but she knew if the prince hadn't taken so much of her blood on her last night in the palace, which left her incoherent, she would have given him far more than just her blood. She would have freely given him her body and her last piece of self-respect.

It was a fact she hated herself for and tried not to think about. Especially since the thought still left her oddly shaken and aching with a need that was left unfulfilled and always would be.

The prince may not have been physically abusive to her, but Max's owner had been just as cruel and brutal as they'd always heard vampires were to their slaves. Only one bite marred Aria's neck, and she'd yearned for it so badly that her whole being had begged for it.

A bite that nearly stripped her soul and left her a far different person than the one she'd been before he fed on her. A mark that was fading faster than she wanted it to, yet nowhere near as soon as she wished it would.

She didn't like losing the mark, it was her last connection to the prince. No matter how much she hated him, she couldn't deny he would always own a piece of her heart. But it could only be a small piece as he had succeeded in shattering the rest of it.

She hoped once the mark was gone she could forget about the prince. Maybe once it was gone, she could move on with her life and not hurt so much all the time. Perhaps she wouldn't ache constantly, the dreams would stop haunting her, and she could end just existing and actually start living again. She would like to take pleasure in the woods again, but since her return, she'd found little joy in the wilderness she'd once loved so dearly.

Max reeled in his line, deftly unhooked a decent sized bass, and added it to their growing catch. Aria pulled up her dark pants, baring her legs to her knees. She squirmed her way closer to the edge of the lake and dipped her legs up to her shins in the water. She would like to go swimming soon, wash her hair, and clean herself.

One of the few things she missed about the palace, besides the prince, was the blessedly hot showers and baths she'd taken. Diving in the lake wasn't the same cleansing experience, though she did it far more often now than before her capture. Being clean every day while in the palace had left her with the same desire now that she was home.

After about an hour, Max finally spoke. "You had another bad dream last night."

Aria sat silently; she didn't know how to tell him she didn't have nightmares like he did. She didn't relive violent beatings and torture. Her dreams were about the last night she had with the prince, the awe she felt, the joy and love suffusing her. His feeding on her was so breathtaking that she still missed the connection—something she would never admit.

It had been painful for Max when his owner drank from him, but for her, it was a moment of pure ecstasy that touched her profoundly. It was the loss of that joy, the loss of *him*, causing her to cry and moan and awaken at night. For her, the night was not about reliving torment like it was with Max, it was about reliving heartache.

She had never deluded herself into thinking anything between her and the prince could last. Eventually, the rest of the royal family, and his *wife*, would have seen to her death.

She *had* deluded herself into thinking he might care for her too. But that was before she learned the prince was already engaged to someone else. The thought still left her feeling furious and betrayed.

Max wrapped his hands lightly around hers, trying to steady them as they shook on the pole. "The fish will know you're here," he said.

She managed to return his weak smile as she labored to breathe, struggled to regain control of her bruised pride and broken heart. "I don't think my nightmares are as bad as yours," she said quietly.

He squeezed her hand soothingly before reluctantly releasing her. They had never spoken about their experiences, though it was apparent they'd both changed forever. But Aria had gained weight while in captivity; Max had grown even thinner, and his bones were still sharp against his pale skin. He had far more bruises, scars, and bite marks than she did, though her scars were mainly inside. His experience was much more physically taxing but just as mentally abusive, and toxic, as hers.

"That's a good thing," he murmured.

She tilted her head, offering him a small half smile. His clear blue eyes were tender. His sandy blond hair hung about his handsome face and stark features. It was her fault Max was in that awful situation. He allowed himself to be captured after she was taken, with the hope he could get them both free.

Unfortunately, he hadn't anticipated how locked down blood slaves were. Though, she'd been afforded far more freedom than him.

She glanced at her wrist, the one scarred by the leash she'd tried to rip from her. All she'd gotten for her efforts was a bloody wrist, bloody fingers, and a pissed off prince who had been unbelievably tender afterward.

She forcefully shut down the thought. Recalling the prince as tender and loving only reopened the raw and jagged lesions still festering on her heart.

"You never should have been there, Max, I'm sorry," she said.

It was the first time she'd apologized to him for her role in his capture; she couldn't get the words out before. She'd tried to apologize many, *many* times, but neither of them liked to be reminded of their time there.

They both kept it to themselves in a bogus attempt to deny it even happened, and they were both failing miserably at it. No matter how much they sought to pretend their captivity hadn't happened, they couldn't succeed.

He was silent for a moment as he stared across the lake.

When he turned toward her, his eyes were haunted, but there was something else in them too, something more.

Only one other man had ever looked at her like that, and in the end, he'd left her shattered. She was barely able to breathe through the grief continuously clawing at her insides. The prince had ruined her, and Max didn't fully understand that yet. She hoped one day he would. The last thing she wanted was to have Max saddened because of her again, but with the way he was looking at her, she felt it was inevitable.

"I chose to go after you, Aria. It was my fault I was caught, not yours. Even knowing what I do now, I wouldn't change anything. I would never leave you alone, never."

She searched his face. She'd always found him handsome, and she still did, but it was not the dark, dangerous ruggedness the prince possessed. Max was blond, with bright blue eyes, and his open, sweet face made many girls swoon.

At one time, he'd made *her* swoon. So much so that Max was her first and only kiss before she met the prince. And then she'd known that no matter what feelings she once possessed for Max, they'd been nothing compared to what she felt for the prince.

And now the prince was gone, lost to her forever. Max was looking at her with the same amount of longing she'd seen in the eyes of the prince. She swallowed the lump in her throat, fighting against the tears threatening to fall. Unlike the prince though, Max would never betray or use her.

Max would love her and never seek to destroy her. He would do everything in his power to keep her safe, to build her up again, and would sacrifice himself over and over for her. Even if the prince *could* locate her, he never would come for her. The prince had a fiancée to take care of now, a vampire to build a life with, to have children with. She was nothing but a pitiful human toy to him.

Even knowing all these things, why did she still love the

bastard? Why on earth couldn't she love someone as caring and sweet as Max? Oddly enough, she did love Max. She loved him with a fierce sort of protective love, but she wasn't *in* love with Max and knew she never would be.

Aria shook her head, trying to deny his words. "Max—"

"It's okay, Aria, one day you'll forget him, you'll move on."

"You know about him?" she whispered, unexpected shame flooding her body.

She felt like a traitor and a fool. Her father was the leader of the rebels; her brothers and Max were some of his strongest fighters in the cause, just as she was before her capture. They had been willing to risk their lives for her, and she...

Well, she had given her heart to a vampire, the oldest son in the royal family no less, the heir to the throne. They had been willing to die for her while she had been falling in love with one of their greatest enemies. She thought of the prince as a monster, and because she loved him, she'd also come to accept the fact she must be one too.

"I suspected," he murmured. "You can't blame yourself, Aria, it was an awful time. Things were warped and wrong in there. It's not your fault you trusted him. Of course, you did; it was frightening, and you were confused. He had a month to manipulate you, to make you think you could believe in and love him."

"Oh, Max," she breathed.

She wished the explanation was that simple, but she knew it wasn't. The prince hadn't twisted her; he hadn't used her terror and confusion against her. He was kind and caring, and he'd needed her. She knew that. Though he had a fiancée the whole time, at the very least, she knew she'd been a little bit special to him.

But she still should have fought against her feelings more. He was her enemy, he would always be her enemy, and they'd never had a chance at a future. She knew all of that, yet she still offered him her blood with no reservations and no fear.

She'd willingly given him her heart. She hated to pop Max's bubble, but he couldn't go about thinking such things. He had to know she wasn't corrupted in there, but a willing, even *eager*, participant.

He had to know she was a horrible person. Had to know these things so he would stop looking at her like that, and so he would understand she could never care for him the same way he cared for her.

"I'm sorry, Max," she whispered. "But that's not what happened. He didn't manipulate me; he didn't corrupt me. He was kind to me; he took care of me. I may have been his blood slave, but he only treated me as such when it was necessary. I would like to say that I didn't come to care for him, that I remained loyal to you and everyone here, but I can't. I loved him, Max..."

She broke off, unable to speak through the grief clawing at her. "I still love him," she choked out.

He stared at her for a moment, his eyes wide in disbelief, and then he shook his head rapidly. His sandy blond hair fell across his forehead curling around his bright eyes.

"But don't you see, Aria, that *is* how he twisted you. He knew you'd always had nothing and your life was hard. He knew by being kind, by giving you the things you never had, you would come to rely on him, trust him, and perhaps even convince yourself you cared for him. That way it would be more fun when he destroyed you. It's why he never told you he was engaged."

Aria's fingernails clawed into the edge of the river bank as she grasped it. She tried to believe Max's words. Maybe, just maybe, she could move on if she believed them, but she couldn't.

Yes, the prince kept his fiancée from her, yes he was dishonest, and yes he broke her heart, but something between them *had* been real. There had been a strange connection between them from the very beginning. Max was aware the prince was blind; he didn't know that whenever the prince was near *her*, he could see again.

And though the prince omitted things about his life, she knew he wasn't lying about only being able to see around her. The fact he could see her was the reason he had claimed her as his first blood slave.

No, Max didn't know about that, and as far as she was concerned no one ever would, not even the prince's brother, Jack. That secret would stay between them. It was the one secret she clung to; the one idea that made her believe it hadn't all been a lie. It was the only thing helping to ease her self-disgust a little.

Although she knew she would never see or feel him again, and even though he'd hurt her so badly, she needed to believe he'd cared for her, at least a little bit. It probably wasn't the best idea for her to cling to that notion, not when she had to let him go, but she couldn't help it. Right now, it was the only thing getting her through the days.

"I don't think so, Max."

"I do," he replied with more confidence than she had. "And one day you will realize it too. You just need time for his psychological games to wear off, and when they do, I'll be here."

Aria shook her head. "No, Max..."

Her words broke off as he clasped her chin, turning her so she had to face him. He wiped the tears from her face. Tears she hadn't known were falling.

"Yes, Aria," he said.

Before she could react, he leaned forward and kissed her. Aria started in surprise, she didn't know what to do or how to respond, but before she could do anything he was already pulling away from her. She could only sit and stare at him as he smiled back at her.

"Just thought it was time for our second kiss," he said.

She couldn't have disagreed more, but she didn't say so. She was selfish for not telling him that, but she had already lost so much in the past couple of months, she couldn't bear to lose Max's friendship as well. However, once he realized who she truly was, how little she deserved his love, he would turn against her.

"We should be going," she managed to choke out.

Nodding, he climbed to his feet and wiped the dirt and mud off his pants as he went. Aria listened to the familiar sounds of the forest, *her* forest as she followed him. She had always taken solace and refuge within these thick woods, but she couldn't find either of those things as of late.

LEANING against the wall of the cave, Aria stared out the entrance. In the shadows of the evening, she could just barely make out the figures of a few guards, but she only saw them because she knew they were there. If she hadn't known, she would never spot them amongst their strategic hiding spots.

The caves were good shelter, but without fair warning an attack was coming, it was easy to get trapped within the thick walls. There were many escape routes throughout the underground system, but there were just as many dead ends.

She glanced behind her, but the cave was dark. The fires were lit much further beneath the earth, where they couldn't be seen from the woods. She didn't fool herself into thinking she was alone out here; her father had people watching her like a hawk since she was taken, but at least she had a little sense of peace and tranquility. Well, that was until she felt William coming.

She turned as her twin emerged from the dark recesses of the cave. She would know him anywhere and often felt him coming before he arrived. He leaned against the wall opposite her, his arms folded across his chest as he gazed at her.

They both had the same bright blue eyes, the same dark auburn hair. Though they'd come from two different eggs, they were even more similar than most identical twins. Right down to their quick tempers and impulsive actions.

Those impulsive actions were what led her to imprisonment and subsequently being made a blood slave, and though she'd like to say they were both more thoughtful now, she'd be lying. The only thing that had changed was she was sadder and more mature than before going into the palace, and William was angrier.

He blamed himself for not being with her that day, even though he'd been injured and unable to accompany her on the hunt. He hated the vampires for taking her, and he especially hated the prince for claiming her as a blood slave.

She'd tried explaining to all of them she hadn't been abused, that only her heart was maimed, but none of them believed her. She supposed it didn't help she was more like the walking dead than a living person since her return. She most certainly wasn't the same girl taken from these woods, and they blamed the prince for that.

They didn't understand he'd saved her from a fate far worse than the one she'd experienced. It had been another vampire who claimed her initially; if it weren't for the prince, far worse things would have been done to her. Whereas they felt she'd been tortured, she knew she was lucky.

"Do you think you'll ever fall in love?" she questioned.

He turned toward her, his eyes bright in the night, his dark eyebrows quirked upward as he studied her. "Is that what you think you were?"

She was silent as she thought over her next words. She had never kept anything from William, they always shared everything, but he'd been so angry lately that she worried her words might send him over the edge. She couldn't lie to him though.

"Yes," she said.

He ran a hand through his shaggy hair. She could tell he was trying to keep hold of his temper and struggling to hide the vehemence behind his emotion.

"Aria, things happened in there, things I can't even begin to imagine—"

"Don't, William. Max may choose to believe that, but you know better. You know me; you know who I am. Do you think I don't know what I felt in there?"

"I believe you *think* you do."

Aria's hands fisted in frustration; it seemed everyone thought she didn't know her own feelings. But she supposed if it were William telling her these things, she wouldn't believe them either.

"And no, I don't think I will ever fall in love," William said.

"Oh."

He moved away from the wall; throwing his arm casually around her shoulders, he pulled her to his side. He grinned down at her, and she couldn't help but grin back at him. For the first time in their lives, he may not understand her, but he would always love her. No matter what.

She dropped her head to his chest and wrapped her arm around his waist. She listened to the sound of his heart as they stared out at the night. So absorbed in the reassuring beat of his heart, it took her a few moments to realize all the animals and insects had gone silent.

Aria lifted her head slowly; her heart thumped wildly as she gazed at the darkness. She searched for the guards amongst the trees and spotted their prone figures amid the night.

"William," she whispered.

"I know. Come on."

He pushed her deeper into the cave, with his hand on her back, as they made their way swiftly through the familiar terrain. The guards still hadn't raised the alarm, a low pitched whistle that easily blended in with the chirruping of the insects, but Aria strained to hear it. It had to be coming soon.

"Hurry!" A sense of doom descended over her as her breath came faster.

Her hand clenched on William's. When they were far enough from the entrance they broke into a run. Their feet flew over the rock of the cave floor. They might already be too late if the vampires were already on them.

With the vampire's exceptional eyesight in the dark, and their rapid speed, it would be almost impossible for her and William to escape. They took a side tunnel on the right and ducked when the ceiling became lower. William turned back and grabbed one of the substantial iron gates built into the wall.

"The guards!" she hissed, grabbing his arm before he could close the gate.

"It's too late for them, Aria."

Horror filled her as the low pitched warning whistle echoed through the caves. William froze for a moment; the gate was still partly open when she sensed, more than heard, something approaching.

William effectively sealed the guards out as he closed the gate as quietly as possible. Many other tunnels led through here. It could take a while for the vampires to find the right one, and the gate should buy them enough time to attempt an escape.

They retreated, moving as quickly as they could through the stooped tunnel. Aria's heart pounded rapidly in her chest, a crushing sense of time running out seized her as something large and heavy slammed into the gate, rattling it within the frame.

Continue reading *Renegade*, The Captive Series book 2: ericastevensauthor.com/Renwb

Stay in touch on updates and new releases from the author by joining the mailing list:
Mailing list for Erica Stevens & Brenda K. Davies Updates: ericastevensauthor.com/ESBKDNews

FIND THE AUTHOR

Erica Stevens/Brenda K. Davies Mailing List:
ericastevensauthor.com/ESBKDNews

Facebook page: ericastevensauthor.com/ESfb

Erica Stevens/Brenda K. Davies Book Club:
ericastevensauthor.com/ESBKDBookClub

Instagram: ericastevensauthor.com/ESinsta
Twitter: ericastevensauthor.com/EStw
Website: ericastevensauthor.com
Blog: ericastevensauthor.com/ESblog
BookBub: ericastevensauthor.com/ESbkbb

ABOUT THE AUTHOR

Erica Stevens is the author of the Captive Series, Coven Series, Kindred Series, Fire & Ice Series, Ravening Series, and the Survivor Chronicles. She enjoys writing young adult, new adult, romance, horror, and science fiction. She also writes adult paranormal romance and historical romance under the pen name, Brenda K. Davies. When not out with friends and family, she is at home with her husband, son, dog, cat, and horse.

BOOKSHELF

Books written under the pen name

Erica Stevens

The Coven Series

Nightmares (Book 1)

The Maze (Book 2)

Dream Walker (Book 3)

The Captive Series

Captured (Book 1)

Renegade (Book 2)

Refugee (Book 3)

Salvation (Book 4)

Redemption (Book 5)

Vengeance (Book 6)

Unbound (Book 7)

Broken (Book 8)

The Captive Series Prequel

The Kindred Series

Kindred (Book 1)

Ashes (Book 2)

Kindled (Book 3)

Inferno (Book 4)

Phoenix Rising (Book 5)

The Fire & Ice Series

Frost Burn (Book 1)

Arctic Fire (Book 2)

Scorched Ice (Book 3)

The Ravening Series

The Ravening (Book 1)

Taken Over (Book 2)

Reclamation (Book 3)

The Survivor Chronicles

The Upheaval (Book 1)

The Divide (Book 2)

The Forsaken (Book 3)

The Risen (Book 4)

Books written under the pen name
Brenda K. Davies

The Vampire Awakenings Series

Awakened (Book 1)

Destined (Book 2)

Untamed (Book 3)

Enraptured (Book 4)

Undone (Book 5)

Fractured (Book 6)

Ravaged (Book 7)

Consumed (Book 8)

Unforeseen (Book 9)

Forsaken (Book 10)

Relentless (Book 11)

Legacy (Book 12)

Coming 2021

The Alliance Series

Eternally Bound (Book 1)

Bound by Vengeance (Book 2)

Bound by Darkness (Book 3)

Bound by Passion (Book 4)

Bound by Torment (Book 5)

Bound by Danger (Book 6)

Coming 2020

The Road to Hell Series

Good Intentions (Book 1)

Carved (Book 2)

The Road (Book 3)

Into Hell (Book 4)

Hell on Earth Series

Hell on Earth (Book 1)

Into the Abyss (Book 2)

Kiss of Death (Book 3)

Edge of the Darkness (Book 4)

Historical Romance

A Stolen Heart